"Stay away from James. He's not your type!"

Dane's tone was as sharp as his words. "James is too much of a loser for a self-seeking little witch like you...."

Lisa shrank at the unfairness of his statement. "May I go now?" she asked faintly. "Or do you have more insults to fling at me?"

"The truth hurts, does it?" Dane asked inimically.

"The truth?" she echoed. "What would you know about that?"

"I know all about you, Lisa. You almost fooled me—" he hesitated "—but that doesn't matter now."

"How right you are!" she flashed. "Your opinion of me couldn't matter less." But it was a lie. Dane's opinion of her had mattered more than anything two years ago. Sadly Lisa had to admit that some things don't change with time....

SARA CRAVEN
is also the author of these

Harlequin Presents

and this
Harlequin Romance

Many of these titles are available at your local bookseller.

For a free catalogue listing all available Harlequin Romances
and Harlequin Presents, send your name and address to:

HARLEQUIN READER SERVICE,
1440 South Priest Drive, Tempe, AZ 85281
Canadian address: Stratford, Ontario N5A 6W2

SARA CRAVEN

dark summer dawn

Harlequin Books

TORONTO • LONDON • LOS ANGELES • AMSTERDAM
SYDNEY • HAMBURG • PARIS • STOCKHOLM • ATHENS • TOKYO

Harlequin Presents edition published March 1982
ISBN 0-373-10487-1

Original hardcover edition published in 1981
by Mills & Boon Limited

CHAPTER ONE

SHE was so bone-weary that she could hardly fit her key into the lock of the front door. It had been a long and turbulent flight, and the landing had been delayed through fog. One of the younger girls had become almost hysterical with fright, and it had been Lisa who had sat with her and soothed her while the plane made its ultimate, laborious descent.

She closed the door behind her thankfully and stood for a moment, staring round the living room. It was scrupulously clean and tidy—Mrs Hargreaves had seen to that—but the air smelled stale and unused. Lisa opened the window and let the January evening air stream into the room.

Her body shivered a little, still nostalgic for the sultry heat of the Caribbean sun she had just left, but her tired mind welcomed the invigoration of the icy draught.

A pile of mail awaited her attention on the small dining table by the window, and she had picked up more envelopes from the mat on her way through, but that could wait until tomorrow, she thought, kicking her shoes off. She needed a bath too. She felt cramped and sticky after the long hours in the plane, and then the taxi ride, crammed in with the other girls—but that could wait as well.

She walked into the bedroom, shedding her clothes as she went. The bed waited, its covers invitingly turned back, and her nightdress arranged in a fan shape, because Mrs Hargreaves had once been a chambermaid in a hotel, but Lisa didn't even bother with that. She simply cleaned off her make-up—the routine she would follow if she was dying,

5

she'd often thought—and fell, naked, into bed and into profound sleep.

She stirred once or twice, even opened her eyes, disturbed by noises in the street outside, a vacuum cleaner operating in the flat above, but she did not wake. When eventually she moved, stretched luxuriously and sat up, yawning, a glance at her watch showed she had slept the clock round. She thought ruefully, 'I must be getting old.' She'd felt old on the trip. All the other models had been in their teens; she'd been the only twenty-year-old.

Jos had laughed at her. 'Found any grey hairs?' he'd jeered. 'Don't complain to Myra about your age. She's two years older than you.'

Lisa didn't bother to state the obvious—that Myra was not and never would be a photographic model. She'd been a plump, pretty art student with gentle eyes and a mass of waving hair when Jos had met and married her, and marriage and a baby hadn't changed her, but neither her face nor her figure would ever be her fortune.

Nor are mine, Lisa thought as she got out of bed, but they're a living.

She glanced at herself in the full-length mirror as she padded into the bathroom and turned on the shower. There was nothing narcissistic in the action, but it probably wasn't strictly necessary either. She had been in the West Indies with the others to model a range of very expensive swim-wear for a glossy magazine, and Lisa would soon have heard it from Jos if her slender body had gained or lost a vital pound anywhere. He had known her ever since she came to London looking for work two years before, and he'd taught her all she'd ever needed to know about facing a camera.

Not that she had ever seriously planned to become a model. She had never regarded her own looks as startling in any way, yet it was Jos who had first suggested the idea while she was still at school. He had come to the school to visit his cousin Dinah, who was Lisa's greatest friend, and taken them both out to lunch. He was already a name in the photographic world, and Lisa wouldn't have been human if she hadn't been flattered by his interest, but at the same time she had seen her life running along very different lines.

It had been thanks to Jos that she had earned her first big break when she had been featured as the Amber Girl, advertising a new and exclusive cosmetic range. With her long golden brown hair, and wide hazel eyes which could take on green or golden tones depending on what colour she was wearing, Lisa had been a natural choice on which to centre the campaign. It had been an amazing experience for her. Special exotic costumes in shades of gold and amber had been designed for her, and the effect against the faint honey tan of her skin had been stunning. They had ranged from sinuous and semi-transparent caftans in silks and chiffons to the briefest concessions to decency in gold mesh and beading. Her face had stared from the pages of every glossy magazine, her eyes seeming to widen endlessly, while the delicate mouth curled a little, giving an effect which was at the same time innocent and sensual. The French fashion house which was launching the Amber range had been ecstatic, and sales had boomed.

But Jos had seriously advised her against taking part in any follow-up.

'You'll be typed if you do. Everyone will associate you with Amber and nothing else,' he'd warned. 'That's fine for a while, but what happens when you get tired of it—or they do?'

She had taken his advice and never regretted it, because offers of work had come flooding in. But she liked working with Jos best. He had been the first to recognise her potential, and she would always be grateful for that. She'd been lucky. From stories she had heard from other girls, the fringes of the modelling profession were grubby in the extreme.

Finding the flat had been another piece of luck, she thought, stepping under the shower and letting the warm water cascade through her hair and down her body. It wasn't cheap, but with Dinah, who shared it with her, landing a part in a long-running West End comedy almost as soon as she had left drama school, they had few financial problems.

Lisa reached for the shampoo and began to lather her hair. Her long sleep had done her good, and now she was hungry. Presently she would make herself a meal, and open her letters while she ate and dried her hair. Not that there would be anything very exciting in her mail, she reminded herself. Most homecomings were attended by bills and circulars. But she had other friends, besides Dinah, with whom she maintained an infrequent but faithful correspondence. Clare might have had her baby by now, she reflected, and Frances could have made up her mind whether or not she wanted that job in the States.

She rinsed her hair and turned off the shower. She dried herself and put on an elderly white towelling bathrobe. It wasn't a glamorous piece of nightwear, but it was reasonably cosy for the sort of evening she had in mind, relaxing by the fire and maybe later listening to a radio play.

Mrs Hargreaves had stocked the fridge and the vegetable rack on her last visit, so Lisa, a towel swathed round her wet hair, grilled herself a steak and made a salad to go with it.

She hadn't an enormous appetite—it had been something which had alarmed her stepfather when she had first gone to live at Stoniscliffe. 'Doesn't eat enough to keep a fly alive,' he'd grumbled at each mealtime. But she liked simple food, well cooked, and was thankful she didn't have to fight a weight problem.

When she had eaten and cleared away, she carried her coffee over to the sofa and curled up with her letters. As she had suspected, most of them were in buff envelopes, and she grimaced slightly as she turned them over. And then she saw there was a letter from Julie.

Lisa stared down at the square white envelope, and the familiar sprawling handwriting, her brows drawing together in a swift frown. Instinct told her that Julie would only be writing to her because of some kind of crisis, and reminded her that it would probably be something she would rather not know about. Such knowledge in the past had always worked to her disadvantage.

Unless it was about Chas, she thought, a sudden feeling of panic seizing her. He hadn't been well, she knew from his own rare letters, and it had been a while since she'd heard from him, apart from the usual formal exchange of cards at Christmas.

She went on looking at the unopened envelope, concern for Chas battling with a desire to tear Julie's letter into small pieces unread. She owed her young stepsister nothing, she thought vehemently. In fact, the boot was very much on the other foot.

But Chas was different. She had never met with anything but kindness and consideration from him, and she owed him something in return. Oh, not the money he had paid into her bank account each quarter, she thought fiercely, although she could have repaid it easily because she never touched it. When she had left Stoniscliffe, she had sworn she would never accept another penny of Riderwood money. She would be independent of them all, especially . . . .

She stopped abruptly, closing her mind, wiping it clean like an unwanted tape. She tried not to think of Stoniscliffe ever, because it was forbidden territory to her now.

She had promised herself she would never go back, although her conscience would not allow her to lose all contact with Chas who had been deeply wounded by her decision to leave. And the awful truth was it had been impossible to tell him why she had to go.

Slowly and reluctantly she opened the envelope and extracted the sheet of notepaper inside.

'Darling Lisa.' Julie's exuberant writing straggled halfway across the page. 'Guess what? I'm going to be married! I'm actually going to amaze everyone and do the right thing for once. It's Tony Bainbridge, of course, and Father is over the moon. The wedding is next month, and I want you to be my bridesmaid—maid of honour—what the hell! Please, please say you will, darling. The arrangements are driving me up the wall already, and Mama Bainbridge is threatening to take over. Please come home, Lisa. I need you. Surely you can have some time off. I'll expect to hear from you. Love, Julie.'

The crunch came at the end, obviously scribbled as an afterthought. 'Dane, of course, is going to give me away.'

Lisa sat very still, staring down at the sheet of paper, then her hand closed convulsively on it, reducing it to a crumpled ball.

She said aloud, 'No,' and then raising her voice slightly, 'God, no!'

She was shivering suddenly and she pulled the dressing gown further around her, and turned the gas fire full on, just as if the chill which had enveloped her was a purely physical one and could be dispelled by such homely means.

Running her tongue round dry lips, she made herself think of Julie. Of Julie going to be married to the young man Chas had always hoped would be her husband. Julie's decision might not amaze everyone as she had jokingly predicted, but Lisa found it hard to accept, just the same. It had been two years since she'd seen Julie, and she supposed her stepsister could have matured considerably in that time. But remembering the young, wild Julie she had always known, it seemed almost incredible.

She tried to remember Tony Bainbridge. He had always been there when they were growing up, because his father owned the neighbouring estate, but he had never made a very lasting impression on Lisa. He was fair, she thought, pleasant and undeniably wealthy. Quite a catch for most girls. But for Julie, daughter of a wealthy industrialist herself—spoiled, wilful Julie?

Lisa moved her shoulders wearily. Well, love sometimes made strange matches. And surely Julie, young, beautiful vibrant Julie, with her mass of dark curling hair, must be marrying for love, and not just because she knew that such a marriage had always been the sentimental wish of both families. Not even Julie would give way to such a mad impulse, she argued with herself, but she was not convinced.

Unwillingly, she smoothed out the letter and re-read it, trying to ignore the postscript. It was Julie's usual breath-less style, sprinkled with underlinings and exclamation marks, but was it the letter of a radiantly happy bride-to-be?

She closed her eyes. Since she was ten years old and had first gone to live at Stoniscliffe, she had protected Julie. That first night, still bewildered by the speed with which everything had happened, and struggling with the un-familiarity of a strange bed in a strange room, she had been startled when her door opened. Julie had said plaintively, 'Mrs Arkwright says I'm too old for a nightlight, but I'm *frightened* of the dark. May I get in with you? Please, Lisa, please!'

Lisa had spent an uncomfortable night. The bed wasn't big enough for two and Julie wriggled. Next day Chas had roared with laughter, totally dismissing the housekeeper's disapproval, and ordered Julie's bed to be moved into Lisa's room.

'Told you, didn't I?' He turned to Lisa's mother, his face beaming. 'Told you they'd be sisters.'

Jennifer Riderwood had nodded, her eyes faintly troubled. Because she knew that having to share a room for the first time was only one of many adjustments Lisa would have to make in her new life.

She had been a widow for five years when she had had that unexpected Premium Bond win, and it couldn't have happened at a better time. She hadn't any particular skills. There was no career for her to fall back on when she was left alone with a small child to bring up. She had to take what work she could, and be thankful. She had to be thankful too that they had a roof over their heads, even if it did belong to her sister-in-law and her husband.

Clive and Enid Farrell were quite aware that it had been good of them to take Jennifer and her child into their home. After all, they'd been under no actual *obligation*, as they stressed whenever the subject was mentioned. They made it seem as if it had been a gesture of pure kindness, and only they and Jennifer knew that she paid a generous rent in order to be made to feel like a poor relation.

Yet it was never enough. Some of Lisa's earliest memories were of hearing Aunt Enid complaining about inflation and rising prices. She'd had to learn to remember to switch off every light—'Wasting electricity' and how many inches of water were permissible at bathtime—'Hot water has to be paid for, my girl.' And she saw her mother's face grow daily more defeated and tired.

Eventually Jennifer had to supplement her wages as a filing clerk by taking an evening job as a waitress, rarely arriving home before midnight. But basically she was a fragile woman and finally, inevitably she collapsed and had to be brought home, and Lisa could remember how angry Aunt Enid had been. There'd been much twitching of net curtains in the street of semi-detached houses where they lived as Jennifer had been carried up the path, and there'd been talk as well, because even as a child, Lisa had recognised that her aunt and uncle were not particularly liked by their neighbours.

But she had been forced to send for the doctor, and Dr Chalmers had spoken bluntly to Jennifer. 'You need a break, my dear. A complete rest, well away from all this—yes, even away from your daughter. It won't hurt her to do without you for a little while. I'm sure that would be her choice, rather than have to do without you permanently.'

There was no money for any kind of holiday. There would be even less money, now that Jennifer had to give up her evening job, so the Premium Bond seemed like a small miracle. It wasn't a fortune, but it was enough to buy Lisa and herself some new clothes, and book a cruise in the Mediterranean—this on Dr Chalmers' advice—and even have some left over for a rainy day.

Looking back, Lisa realised how grateful she and her mother should have been to the doctor who had practically frogmarched her mother round to the travel agency. He had known the Farrells for many years, and was quite well aware of the sort of pressure Jennifer would have to suffer unless she used her win for her own benefit.

As it was, there had been outraged glances and muttered remarks about 'bone selfishness and greed.' There were repairs needed to the roof of Number Thirty-Seven, and they'd thought that Jennifer might like to help—as it was her roof too.

But this time Jennifer was not going to allow herself to be bullied. She had booked her cruise and paid for it, and she was going to take it. And when it was over, and she was back with them, things were never the same again. It wasn't just the fact that she was relaxed and sun-tanned and had put on some weight. There were other, subtler differences— a depth to her smile, and a dreaming look in her eyes when she thought she was unobserved.

And then Charles Riderwood had arrived at the house, tall, powerfully built, a square bluff face lent distinction by the greying hair at his temples.

He had smiled down at Lisa. 'Hello, love.' There was a faint North-country burr underlying his voice. 'I've got a little girl, a couple of years younger than you.'

Lisa had smiled back a little uncertainly, but she had recognised the kindness in his eyes, and she also realised that he wanted her to like him, although she didn't understand why.

Enlightenment was to come after his Jaguar car had driven away.

'Brazen!' Enid Farrell had stormed. 'The very idea, allowing your—fancy man to come here. How dare you!'

Jennifer had flushed, but her voice had been calm. 'Before you say any more, Enid, perhaps you ought to know that Charles and I are going to be married.'

'Married?' Enid's voice had risen almost to a shriek. 'A man you met on a cruise? Why, you know nothing about him. He could be married already—up to no good.'

Jennifer's face had blossomed into a smile. 'I know enough,' she said. 'He's a widower. His wife died several years ago. He has a son of twenty-four and a daughter of eight. His work is something to do with electronics, and he lives in Yorkshire. Is there anything else you want to know?'

Enid Farrell looked outraged. 'Why is the son so much older?' she demanded accusingly.

'I don't know. Perhaps the little girl was an afterthought.'

Enid's face had become more grimly disapproving than ever. It was clear she considered that after sixteen years people should be thinking of other things.

She continued to disapprove right up to the day of the wedding. Apart from Lisa, she and her husband were the only guests from Jennifer's side. But there were a number of people at the register office who knew Charles Riderwood, and obviously liked him, and they all went on afterwards to the champagne reception he had arranged at the London hotel where he had a suite.

Someone was waiting for them there, a tall dark young man who rose slowly from one of the sofas and stood waiting, his hands resting lightly on his hips.

Charles had said on a sharp note of pleasure, 'Dane, you managed to get here after all!' He turned to Jennifer. 'Come and meet your new son. He's been in America on a post-graduate course or you'd have met him before.'

Dane Riderwood had said lightly, 'It all goes to show I should never turn my back for a minute.' He had stepped forward to shake Jennifer's hand, and there had been a general laugh, but Lisa, hanging back hesitantly, had known instinctively that this stranger who was her step-brother wasn't amused. He was smiling, but his smile never reached his eyes. And when Charles drew Lisa forward, his hand warm and heavy on her shoulder, Dane's eyes flickered over her with an indifference bordering on hostility. He had turned away almost at once, leaving Lisa thinking, 'I don't like him—and he doesn't like us.'

She heard her mother say to her new husband, 'He's very like you,' and she wanted very badly to cry out a denial, because surely Jennifer knew—could see that they weren't a bit alike.

Oh, they were both tall and very dark, but Dane was a much leaner version of his burly father. His face was thinner too, its lines arrogant where Charles' were genial. His eyes weren't blue like his father's either, but a wintry grey, and his mouth was hard.

She had been looking forward to seeing Stoniscliffe, the big grey stone house which her stepfather had told her about. She wanted to meet Julie too.

'She's been lonely for someone to play with,' Chas had

told her. 'I daresay you've been a bit lonely too.'

But all the excitement, all the anticipation she had been feeling had been dampened by the arrival of this cold hostile stranger. She wasn't sure she even wanted to go north to Stoniscliffe if he was going to be there.

She tried to forget about Dane Riderwood and enjoy the reception. People spoke kindly to her, and exclaimed admiringly about her long hair. Chas even gave her a sip of champagne, in spite of her mother's laughing expostulations.

She was just beginning to enjoy herself when Aunt Enid came towards them. Jennifer and Lisa were standing on their own for a moment and she had obviously seized her opportunity.

'Well, you've certainly done all right for yourself,' she hissed to Jennifer. 'Something to do with electronics indeed! You forgot to mention that he owned his own factory. I suppose you'll be off north with never a backward glance, never a thought for the people who fed you and housed you when you had nothing.'

Lisa saw her mother go pale, saw all the pretty, happy, excited colour fade from her face. She said in a low voice, 'Enid, please keep your voice down. I don't expect you to believe me, but I didn't know until today. Oh, I knew Chas wasn't on the breadline, but all this—' she paused and gave a little painful laugh—'all this was as big a shock to me as it has been to you.'

'Oh, of course,' Enid Farrell sneered. 'We always knew we weren't good enough for you. Even my poor brother wasn't that. You always did fancy yourself, with your airs and graces—too good to work or to want. Well, you'll never have to bother about either again!'

Lisa flinched. There was real venom in Aunt Enid's voice. It wasn't just the habitual carping that she and her mother had silently learned to accept. And she had noticed something else too. Dane Riderwood was standing not too far away and judging by the expression of distaste on his face he had heard the tail end if not all of the sordid little passage.

She thought resentfully, 'I wish he hadn't heard. He doesn't like us anyway, and now he'll just think that we're as horrible as *she* is.'

She saw her stepfather coming towards them, beaming, and Aunt Enid moved away then, and not long after that Lisa was relieved to see her and Uncle Clive leaving. All of a sudden she was glad she was going to Stoniscliffe because it meant, she hoped, that she would never see either of them again.

The reception seemed to go on for ever, and Lisa was tired of the new faces and voices going on endlessly above her head. After a while she wandered into the adjoining bedroom. There was a sofa there too, drawn across the window, and she curled up on it, lulled by the distant noise of traffic and the murmur of talk and laughter in the next room.

She didn't know what woke her, but she opened her eyes, blinking drowsily to realise she was no longer alone in the room.

Somewhere near at hand a man's voice was saying, 'Bit of a surprise to all of us, actually. He didn't tell you?'

'Not a word, until it was too damned late for me to do anything about it.' It was Dane Riderwood's voice, molten with fury. 'My God, it's sheer lunacy! He takes a holiday and comes back with some gold-digging little typist and her brat. Heaven knows no one expects him to live like a monk, but surely he didn't have to pay for his fun with marriage!'

Lying, hidden by the high back of the sofa, Lisa felt sick. She didn't understand all that was being said, but she could recognise the cold contempt in 'typist and her brat'. She wanted to jump up and run to Dane Riderwood, to punch him and kick him, and make him sorry, but even as the thought crossed her mind, caution followed. If she did so then other people would come, and they would ask her why she was behaving like that, and she would have to tell them, and her mother's happy, shining day would be spoiled, some instinct told her. Aunt Enid had been bad enough, but this was a hundred times worse.

This was her new family of which Dane was to be an important part, and he didn't like them. He didn't want them. She buried her face in the cushion and put her hands over her ears. She didn't want to hear any more.

She was quiet some time later when Chas and Jennifer came to fetch her, to take her up north to Stoniscliffe. They were having a delayed honeymoon, because Chas wanted to show Jennifer his home, and wanted Lisa to settle in there too.

They looked at her pale cheeks and the wariness in her eyes and decided privately that it was over-excitement and nervousness, and didn't press her for any explanations. It had been a relief to know from chance remarks they had let fall that Dane wouldn't be joining them at Stoniscliffe. He was going back to America.

Perhaps he'll stay there, the child Lisa had thought passionately. Perhaps he'll never come back.

The woman she had become could smile wryly at such naïveté, looking back across the years. Of course he had come back, and gradually the situation had begun to ease although Lisa told herself she could never like him or even wholly trust him, and she was slightly on her guard all the time when he was around.

Grudgingly, she had to give Dane his due. He had never, she was sure, given her mother any distress by even hinting at his true feelings about his father's second marriage. But then he had no reason to do so, she reminded herself. Chas and Jennifer had been very happy—even someone as prejudiced as Dane would have been forced to admit that. He was always civil, if rather aloof, to Jennifer, and he took hardly any notice of Lisa at all. But then, she thought, he had never bothered with Julie either, who had always shown a strong tendency to hero-worship him.

Sisterly devotion had never been Dane's style, Lisa thought with a curl of her lips. He had girl-friends, of course—a lot of them. Some of them even came to stay at Stoniscliffe to run the gauntlet of Chas's indulgently critical appraisal. But it was clear they were for amusement only. Dane showed no signs of becoming serious about any of them, although they were all beautiful and glossy and self-assured—good wife material for a man who stood to inherit a thriving family firm and would need a smooth and practised hostess in his private life.

Julie and Lisa discussed the girls between themselves, tearing their appearances, their manners, their clothes apart mercilessly. Later, they wondered about their sexual potential as well, with avid adolescent curiosity. At least Julie had done most of the wondering. Lis wasn't that interested in the partners Dane chose for his sexual athletics, although she had little doubt he was an expert in that as he was at everything else.

Locally, he was the golden boy, already managing director of Riderwoods which was expanding rapidly and surely. Chas was proud of him, calling him a chip off the old block, but Lisa thought there was more to it than that, unless the original block had been granite, because there was a ruthlessness about Dane that chilled her.

That was why, quite apart from the original dislike and distrust, she had never been able to accord him the admiration which Julie lavished on him. He wasn't Lisa's idea of a hero. She saw no warmth in him, no tenderness.

Even when she was sixteen, and Jennifer who hadn't been well for some time had died very suddenly in her sleep, there had been no softening in him. He had been away on a business trip, but he came home for the funeral, but even while he had uttered his condolences to her, she had the feeling that his thoughts were elsewhere. She had wanted to scream at him, 'You're not sorry! You never wanted her here, or me either.' All the old hostility and hurt had welled up inside her, and she had said something in a cold, quiet little voice and turned away.

She had thought then that she couldn't possibly dislike him more than she did at that moment. But she knew better now.

She leaned back against the sofa cushions, trembling a little inside as she always did when she let herself think of the events of two years before. Not that she often thought of them—the mental censorship she exercised saw to that.

She wouldn't have been thinking of him now—God knows she never wanted to think of him again—if it hadn't been for Julie's letter. '*Dane, of course, is going to give me away.*'

She would have to write to Julie, maybe not tomorrow, but some time soon, and make some excuse. Because there was no way she was ever going back to Stoniscliffe while Dane was there, and Dane was always there now. It was a grief to her. She missed Chas, and the big grey house on the edge of the Dales, but she had to keep away because she never wanted to see or speak to Dane Riderwood again.

The ring at the doorbell made her start, because she wasn't expecting visitors, although there were any number of people who would know she was back from the West Indies by now and could be dropping in. She grimaced slightly at the thought of her appearance, no make-up and hair tied up in a turban, and was strongly tempted not to answer it, but the bell rang again imperatively, and there was little point in pretending she wasn't at home when the caller could see the light shining under the door.

Pushing the litter of papers and envelopes off her lap, she called, 'All right, I'm coming!'

She was smiling a little as she opened the door, because it was more than probably Simon who had shown signs of becoming besotted with her just before she had flown off on this last assignment, and she liked Simon even if she was a long way from falling in love herself.

She began, 'You've caught me at a bad moment. I'm . . .'

And then she stopped, the words dying on her lips as she saw exactly who it was, standing on her doorstep, waiting for admittance.

'Hello, Lisa,' said Dane Riderwood.

CHAPTER TWO

FOR a moment she could neither speak nor move, and her breathing felt oddly constricted. It was like a nightmare—as if Dane was some demon that her thoughts had conjured up. All these months she had never allowed herself to think about him at all, she had closed him out, incised him from her brain.

Now Julie's letter had reluctantly forced open the floodgates of her memory, and she had walked through the past like some forbidden city. 'Talk of the devil,' people used to say, 'and he's sure to appear.' And it was true because the devil was here with her now.

She made a grab for the door intending to slam it in his face, but her momentary hesitation had been her undoing, because he had already forecast her intention and walked into the room.

He said, 'Allow me.' And he closed the door himself, shutting them in together.

Lisa said between her teeth, 'Get out of here!'

'When I'm ready.' His voice was as cool as ever. He had hardly changed at all physically from the first time she had set eyes on him. The lines on his face had deepened with maturity, but his body still had the spare lithe grace of some predatory animal. He moved forward and she recoiled instinctively. He threw back his head and stared at her for a moment, his eyes hooded, their expression enigmatic.

'Relax,' he advised caustically. 'The sooner you hear what I have to say, the sooner I can be gone, which is what we both want.'

'What the hell are you doing here?' she almost whispered.

'I'm not preparing to carry out the fell purposes you seem to have in mind,' he snapped back at her. 'For God's sake, Lisa, sit down and behave like a civilised human being.'

'What would you know about civilised behaviour?' She was beginning to tremble inwardly and she folded her arms defensively across her body. 'Just say whatever you came to say and get out.'

'Ever the gracious hostess.' Dane walked past her, looked with a lift of his eyebrow at the littered sofa, then sat down in the chair opposite. 'You're very nervous,' he commented. 'What's the matter? You said I'd called at a bad moment when you opened the door. Are you—entertaining?' His eyes went over her derisively, establishing beyond doubt that he knew quite well she was naked under the old towelling robe, and she flushed angrily.

'No, I'm not,' she grated, and could have kicked herself. Perhaps if she'd lied and said, 'Yes—someone's waiting for me in the bedroom right now,' he might have left.

'Then I'm fortunate to find you alone,' he said smoothly. 'I'd like some coffee.'

For a moment Lisa stood glaring at him impotently, then she turned and went into the small kitchen. The towel round her hair was slipping and she tore it off impatiently, thrusting it into the small linen basket next to the washing machine. Her hands were shaking so much she could hardly spoon the coffee into the percolator. She began to set a tray with brown pottery mugs, pouring creamy milk into a matching jug. She heard a slight sound behind her, and glancing over her shoulder, realised that Dane was standing in the doorway watching her.

'Do you have sugar?' She made her voice cool and social.

'You've a bad memory, Lisa,' he said sardonically. 'How many years did we live under the same roof, and how many cups of coffee did you pour for me? No, I don't have sugar, and never have done.'

'Too many,' she muttered.

'Well, that's one thing at least we can agree on,' he said. He strolled forward, trapping her between his body and the worktop behind her. He put out a hand and tilted her chin, studying her face critically.

His touch sent every nerve-ending in her body screaming. She wanted to strike his hand away. She wanted to use her nails and teeth to free herself like a cornered animal, but it would be no good, she knew. He was the stronger, and he would not hesitate to use his strength.

He said silkily, 'You don't change, do you, Lisa? I remember you all those years ago—a little hostile creature, all hair and eyes.'

She smiled, a little meaningless stretching of her lips. 'How odd you should say that. I was thinking much the same about you. Oh, not the hair, of course, but the hostility —and the eyes. They haven't altered at all. They're still cold.'

As cold and as cruel as January, she silently added, meeting their greyness, noticing how their bleak light remained unsoftened by the heavy fringing of dark lashes.

Dane said, 'Cold?' and smiled. 'Is that what you really think? Surely not.'

Her breathing quickened a little. 'You wouldn't like to hear what I really think. Now if you want this coffee, you'd better let me make it.'

He flung up his hands in mock capitulation and moved away, and Lisa felt limp with relief.

When she carried the tray through to the living room, he had resumed his seat by the fire and was smoking a cigar. She felt a sudden surge of nostalgia as the scent of the smoke reached her. Chas had always smoked cigars and their faint aroma had hung round the house at Stoniscliffe whenever he was there, as if it was Christmas every day,

Jennifer had said, laughing.

She put the tray down. 'What happened to the cigarettes?'

'I gave them up about eighteen months ago.' He gestured to the cigar. 'Do you object to this?'

'No, of course not.' She subdued an impulse to add it was the least objectionable thing about him, and poured the coffee instead. 'Why do you ask?'

He gave a slight shrug. 'It doesn't fit in with the image here. A masculine intrusion into a purely feminine environment.' He paused. 'Or at least that's the assumption I'm making. Perhaps I'm wrong.'

'Perhaps you are,' she agreed.

He glanced around, brows lifted. 'You don't live alone?'

'I don't live alone.'

Dane was very still for a moment, then he moved abruptly, tapping a sliver of ash from the tip of the cigar. 'Of course not. May one ask where he is?'

'No, I don't think so,' she said calmly. 'Perhaps now you'd like to tell me what you want from me.'

'Not a thing, sweetheart—now or ever.' His voice bit. 'Let's get that firmly established, shall we? I haven't come blundering in on your idyll on my behalf but on Julie's.'

'Julie's?' She was startled, her eyes flying to the creased letter.

His gaze followed hers and his mouth tightened. 'It looks as if I've made a wasted journey. Nevertheless I'll say what I've come to say. Julie's panicking because she hasn't heard from you. She's desperate for you to come home and help with the wedding. She wants to know why you haven't written or phoned.'

Lisa said, 'I only got her letter today. I've been away— abroad. I only returned yesterday.'

'The contents don't seem to have impressed you very much.' Dane was leaning back in the chair, watching her from beneath lowered lids.

'You and I both know,' she said tautly, 'that there is no way I'm ever going back to Stoniscliffe. You'll have to stall Julie—find some explanation that will satisfy her.'

'I can't think of one,' he said. 'And even if I could, I doubt if it would satisfy Chas. He can't wait for you to come—back.'

She noted ironically the small hesitation and wondered whether the word he'd stumbled over had been 'home'.

'How is he?' She wasn't merely trying to change the angle of the subject under discussion. She really wanted to know. Letters were pretty unrevealing, and she had kept hers amusing and busy, providing excuse after excuse for not returning to Yorkshire.

'If you really wanted to know, you would have gone to see for yourself,' Dane said harshly. 'How the hell do you hink he is—trapped in a wheelchair for the rest of his life!'

'A wheelchair?' She gaped at him, her head reeling in disbelief. 'What do you mean?'

'He had a stroke,' Dane said curtly. 'It's left him partly paralysed. He can walk a few yards with difficulty and use one hand.'

Lisa shook her head. 'He said he hadn't been well, but he never even hinted . . .'

'Why should he? If you'd cared, you'd have gone to see.'

'That's your reasoning, not his.' She glared at him.

'Perhaps,' he said. 'He always was too soft with you—too ready to make excuses. He wouldn't write and ask you to come back because he's terrified of pity. He's a strong man who's suddenly found a physical weakness he can't command or overcome, and it's been a struggle for him. He has a nurse living in, but he doesn't ask for help or sympathy from anyone else. He's counting on Julie's wedding to bring you back to Stoniscliffe. I could have told him it was a forlorn hope.'

'That's not true!' Her throat felt thick and tight. 'I—I love Chas.'

'So you've always protested. According to you, you asked for nothing better than to be a daughter to him and a sister to Julie. Well, now's your chance. Live up to your words.'

'It isn't as easy as you think.' She was arguing against herself now, not him, although he wasn't to know that. 'I have a career—commitments.'

'As you've already made clear.' His mouth twisted a little. 'Couldn't you convince him that you also have a commitment to Chas—a prior commitment? Unless, of course, you no longer see it that way. As for your so-called career,' he shrugged, 'I imagine it would survive a slight hiccup like Julie's wedding.'

'You can sneer all you want,' she said furiously, 'but it's my life. It isn't the sort of success you would recognise, but I'm happy. What did you expect me to do—become a "little typist" like my mother?'

'When you can capitalise on your considerable assets? Hardly.' Dane looked her over. 'You must have one of the best known faces and bodies in the country. How does the man in your life like having to share you with the fantasies of thousands of others?'

She shifted her head. 'He survives.' She'd deliberately led him to believe that there was such a man, so there was no point in screaming at him that her face and body belonged to herself alone, that in front of the cameras she played the role Jos had written for her, no more no less, and all it needed now was for Dinah, who was away on tour in the Midlands, to walk in and blow the whole stupid pretence sky high.

'I'm sure he does more than that.' His eyes seemed to linger on her mouth, on the deep vee where the lapels of the dressing gown crossed. 'Even with your hair in rats' tails, you're quite something.'

Lisa felt herself shrink inwardly, but there must have been some physical movement as well, because he threw up a hand. 'Don't be alarmed. I said I wanted nothing from you, and I meant it. All I need is your co-operation for a few weeks.' He paused, then added cynically, 'And you won't be out of pocket over it. I'll make it worth your while.'

She said between her teeth, 'How readily you reduce everything to cash terms. You know what you can do with your bloody money!'

'Spare me the righteous wrath,' he drawled. 'I know quite well Chas has been paying out handsomely for the honour of keeping you in the manner to which you've become accustomed. I can't stop him, of course, but perhaps you should remember that there'll come a time when the gravy train will stop permanently.'

And on that day, Lisa thought savagely, it would give her immense satisfaction to return every unspent penny.

She said with assumed lightness, 'You disappoint me. There was I thinking I was set up for life. I shall have to take care I don't lose my looks.'

'I should just take care generally,' he said gently. He put down the pottery mug and stood up. 'Thank you for the coffee. I'm driving back to Yorkshire tomorrow. I'll pick you up around midday.'

'Thanks, but no, thanks,' she said. 'I have arrangements to make, and there are trains.'

'So there are,' he agreed. 'But Chas at least would think it strange that we didn't travel together. I don't deny your attractions, but I'm sure there are other models in London.'

'Plenty,' she said flatly.

'Then let's have no more excuses about arrangements.' He gave her a long dispassionate look. 'Play this my way, Lisa, and I'll see to it that you aren't bothered in future. You can come back here after the wedding and live whatever kind of life takes your fancy. I'll see you tomorrow, and don't keep me waiting.'

He didn't seem to expect her to show him out, and she was glad of that because she didn't think her shaking legs would support her. She remained on the sofa staring at the door which had just closed behind him and trying to make sense of the last teeming half hour.

In a moment, she told herself, she would wake up and find she'd been having a bad dream. Whenever there had been nightmares, it had always seemed as if Dane was part of them hovering there somewhere on the fringe of her subconscious.

She hoped very much she would wake up soon. She moved restively and her hand caught her undrunk mug of coffee and spilled it across the hearthrug, and she stared for a moment down at the resultant mess, forcing herself to face reality.

Somehow, without knowing quite how it had happened, she was going back to Stoniscliffe to help with Julie's wedding. She sank her teeth into her lower lip. It was no wonder Dane was such a success in business. No object remained immovable for long under the pressure of his irresistible force. She loathed him!

She cleaned up the spilled coffee while her mind ran round and round like a small animal trapped on a wheel. She could always vanish, she supposed. She had done it once two years ago, and she could do it again. But to do so would be to hurt Julie who didn't deserve it, and more importantly, it would grieve Chas.

Lisa caught her breath at the thought of him in a wheelchair. He had always been such a strong, positive man. This new weakness would irk him terribly, she knew, and found herself wondering exactly when it had happened.

At the same time, she told herself fiercely that she wasn't to feel guilty. If her disappearance from Stoniscliffe had had even a remote connection with Chas's stroke, then Dane would have mentioned it. A mirthless smile curved her mouth. Boy, would he have mentioned it! So she wasn't to blame herself, although she knew that her conscience would trouble her. Chas had been ill and needing her, and she hadn't known. Why hadn't Julie told her? she asked herself almost despairingly, and then shook her head at her own foolishness. Julie would have been obeying orders.

Chas would have wanted her to return to Stoniscliffe under her own steam, at her own wish. He wouldn't take kindly to any sort of pleading on his behalf from anyone. Not even from Dane.

So that was yet another secret she had to keep, because Chas had never known the real reason why she had left Stoniscliffe in the first place, and that was the most import-ant secret of all. No one knew the truth except herself, and the man who had just left her crouched, trembling like a child, in a corner of her own sofa.

She went across to the telephone and dialled Jos's number. Myra answered almost at once, and her voice bubbled down the phone as she recognised Lisa.

'Did you enjoy the trip? Are you worn out? Come to supper tomorrow night and tell me your version.'

'I'd love to, but I can't.' Lisa hesitated. 'Is he in a good mood, Myra?'

'Fair to middling. Why, is there something wrong?'

'In a way. I have to go away for a few weeks, that's all.'

'That'll be enough,' Myra said blankly. 'What's happened?' She paused. 'You're not—ill or anything?'

Lisa guessed the real question behind the tactful words. 'No, nothing like that. I have to go up north to organise a family wedding. My stepsister is getting married, and there's a panic on.'

She could hear Myra talking to someone at the other end, her voice muffled and then Jos spoke.

He said sharply, 'What is all this, Lisa? Myra says you're going up north. You have to be joking!'

'I wish I were.' Lisa rapidly explained about the wedding. 'But there's more to it than that,' she went on. 'I've just found out that my stepfather had a stroke at some time, and that he wants to see me.'

'Oh, hell!' Jos was silent for a moment. 'You realise that all this couldn't be happening at a worse time.'

'Please believe that if I could get out of going, I would,' she said unhappily. 'But they're all the family I've got, and I owe them a great deal. Certainly I owe them this.'

'Then obviously you must go, but for heaven's sake get back as soon as you can. They have short memories in this game,' he said grimly. He paused. 'You said they were all the family you've got. Wasn't there a brother as well? I seem to remember Dinah mentioning him.'

'There was and there is,' she said. 'But I don't regard him as a brother. It was Julie I grew up with.'

'Lucky Julie,' Jos commented. 'Tell the stepfather he did a good job. And phone me as soon as you get back.'

'That's a promise,' Lisa said, and replaced her receiver. Her hand was sweating slightly and she wiped it down the skirt of her dressing gown.

She would have to write to Dinah and she could pay Mrs Hargreaves and give her any necessary instructions in the morning. There was no great problem there.

The towering, the insuperable, the shattering difficulty was getting through, firstly, tomorrow, and then the days after that. If it hadn't been for the wedding she might have been able to do a deal—to say to Dane, 'I want to go back. I want to see Chas, to spend some time with him, and I'll do it on the understanding that you go and stay far away from Stoniscliffe while I'm there.'

But because of Chas's paralysis, Dane was going to give

Julie away. He had to be there, and so there was no bargain to be struck.

Not that Dane struck bargains anyway, she thought. He made decisions and carried them through to his own advantage. If he negotiated, he expected to be on the winning side, and generally was. She had never seen him bested by anyone, although at one time she had dreamed dreams of doing it herself. But not any more. He had shown her brutally and finally that against him, she could not win, and she still had the emotional scars to prove it.

But she wasn't going to think about that now. She couldn't let herself think about that because otherwise she would turn tail and run away somewhere—anywhere, and Dane would know then exactly what he had done to her, and triumph in his knowledge.

She was restless, pacing round the flat like an animal in a cage, and she had to make herself stop, and fetch the hairdryer and sit down and do something about her ill-used hair which was going to dry like a furze bush if she wasn't careful, and contribute nothing to her self-confidence. There was something soothing and therapeutic in sitting there, brushing the warm air through her hair, and restoring it to something like its usual smooth shine. She wished she could smooth out her jitters as easily.

She didn't sleep when she went to bed, but she told herself that she wouldn't have slept anyway. She'd had no exercise or fresh air to make her healthily tired.

There was too much to do in the morning to give her time to think. She packed and tried to eat some breakfast, while she gave a surprised Mrs Hargreaves her instructions. Then she found Dinah's tour schedule and wrote her a hasty explanatory note, addressing it to the current theatre.

She dashed out, posted the letter, and as she walked back from the box on the corner, she saw there was a car parked in the street outside the flat. She lived over a shop—a boutique really where they sold small pieces of antique furniture and jewellery, catering for the connoisseur market, and of course the car could have belonged to one of the said connoisseurs, but somehow she didn't think so.

She stood for a moment, her hands buried in her coat pockets, and stared at it, and wished she was able to turn round and walk away again as fast as she could. It was dark and sleek and shining and looked extremely powerful. It proclaimed money and a quiet but potent aggression.

Dane was waiting at the top of the stairs. He swung impatiently to meet her.

'I was beginning to think you'd run out on me.'

'I had to post a letter.' Lisa despised herself for the defensive note in her voice. She had nothing to apologise for. She wasn't late; he was early. She took her key out of her pocket and Dane calmly appropriated it and fitted it into the lock.

'Thank you,' she said between her teeth, and went past him into the flat.

'If you're ready, I'd like to leave as soon as possible,' he said. 'The weather forecast isn't too good for later in the day.'

It would be brave weather that would dare interfere with his arrangements, she thought bitterly as she went into the bedroom to close her case. She tugged russet suede boots on over her slim-fitting cream cord jeans, and pulled a matching coat, warmly lined, on top of her cream Shetland sweater. She had left her hair hanging loose round her shoulders as she had worked and packed, but now it was a moment's task to sweep it into a smooth coil and anchor it securely on top of her head. It was a severe style, but it suited her, highlighting the line of her cheekbones and her smooth curve of jaw.

She picked up her case and the weekend bag that matched it and went into the living room. Dane was standing by the window looking down into the street.

'Is that all you're taking?' His glance ran over her luggage.

'It's enough,' she returned shortly. 'I've learned to travel lightly.'

'But not alone.' There was a barb in the smooth words which angered her, but she decided to ignore it. The journey ahead was going to be trying enough without a constant sparring match going on between them.

Dane picked up the cases. 'I'll put these in the boot while you see to any locking up you need to do.'

She was fastening the safety catches on the windows when the phone rang.

'Lisa?' Simon Whitman's voice sounded plaintively down the line. 'Jos has just told me you're off up north for an unspecified time. What's going on?'

Her heart sank at the note of grievance in his voice, which she had to admit was fully justified. Before the West Indies assignment, she and Simon had been seeing quite a lot of each other. She had met him some months before through her work, because he was a young and promising executive with an advertising agency which often used Jos's photographs. They had got on well almost immediately, and she had accepted the invitation to dinner from him which had speedily followed. They were starting to be spoken of as a couple, to be invited to places together, and although Lisa wasn't sure that was entirely what she wanted, she was happy enough with the arrangement to allow it to continue unchallenged as long as Simon didn't start making demands she couldn't fulfil. Up to now, he had shown no signs of this. On the contrary, he had seemed quite happy to keep their relationship as light and uncommitted as she could have wished, but just then she had heard a distinctly proprietorial note in his voice.

She said, 'A family emergency of sorts.' She should have

let him know, she thought. He should have been on her list ahead of Dinah and Mrs Hargreaves really, but the truth was she had never even given him a thought. She went on, 'It's been landed on me so suddenly, I haven't really had a chance to contact anyone.'

'I didn't think I was just anyone,' Simon said, and there seemed no answer to that, so Lisa didn't make one. After a pause, he said 'Will you be gone for very long?'

'I hope not,' she said. 'For as long as it takes, and no longer. I do have my living to earn, and as Jos reminded me, they have short memories in the fashion world.'

'They'll remember you.' His voice warmed, lifted a little. 'I can't get you out of my mind, night or day.'

That troubled her a little, but she found herself smiling. 'It would be nice if the other agencies in town felt the same. Do you think you could become contagious?'

She was aware that Dane had come back into the room and was standing by the door, silently watching and listening. Anyone else would have had the decency to withdraw out of earshot, she thought bitterly as she turned a resentful shoulder on him.

She could hardly hear what Simon was saying. She had to force herself to concentrate on his words because she was too conscious of that other dark and disturbing presence behind her.

Simon said with that special note in his voice which belonged to almost everyone who had spent their entire lives south of Potters Bar, 'It will be awful in the north at this time of year, and they reckon there's bad weather on the way. You'll take care, won't you, love?'

Lisa said, 'I can take care of myself.' And froze as she realised what she'd said, the words acting like a key to unlock the secret place in her mind and unleash the nightmares which lurked there. She found she was gripping the phone until her knuckles went white. She answered Simon in monosyllables 'Yes' and 'No', praying that each response was the right one because he might have been talking so much gibberish.

Eventually she said with a kind of insane brightness in her voice, 'Look, I really must go now. I'll see you when I get back.'

Simon said goodbye in his turn. He sounded disappointed, as if for all his warnings about the weather he had hoped she might give him the address she was going to, the telephone number so that he could make contact.

She replaced the receiver on the rest with unsteady fingers, and turned slowly.

Across the room, Dane's eyes met hers, cold and watchful, and she knew that her words had triggered off memories for him too and for an endless moment the past held them in its bleak trap.

If she backed away, he would come after her, a jungle cat stalking his prey. But she had no reason to back off. Because this time what she said was true. She could look after herself, and she would. Neither Dane nor anyone else had the power to harm her.

And sitting beside him in silence, as the car devoured the miles on the motorway, Lisa found herself repeating those words over and over again as if they were an incantation that would keep her safe.

CHAPTER THREE

THEY had been travelling for over an hour and a half when Lisa realised that Dane had signalled his intention of turning off the motorway.

'Where are we going?' she asked sharply.

'To eat. There's a pub I often use not far from here.'

'Must we stop? I'm not particularly hungry.'

'I intend to stop, yes,' he said coolly. 'If you don't want to join me you can always wait in solitary splendour in the car.'

Lisa compressed her lips angrily. She had no intention of doing anything of the kind, as he was perfectly aware.

The village they eventually came to was charming, with well tended houses clustering round a green and a duck-pond. The inn, set back from the road, was a long low building, whitewashed and spruce, and there were already several cars parked at the rear.

Lisa fumbled with the catch on the passenger door, trying desperately to release it while Dane attended to the security on the driver's side, but it resisted all her efforts, and to her annoyance Dane had to come round and open the door from the outside. For a moment she was afraid he was going to help her out. She didn't want him to touch her, and she scrambled out with none of her usual grace, bitterly aware of the slight mocking smile which twisted his mouth.

As they walked towards the inn door, a large Alsatian came round the corner of the building. He paused when he saw them, his ears cocked inquisitively, the long plumy tail beginning to wave slightly.

'What a beauty!' Lisa exclaimed impulsively, and put out

her hand. The dog came up and sniffed at her fingers, then allowed his head to be gently scratched.

'You never learn, do you, Lisa?' Dane said harshly. He took her hand and turned it palm upwards, pointing to a faint white mark. 'Didn't Jeff Barton's collie teach you anything?'

Lisa flushed as she pulled her hand away. It had been her first summer at Stoniscliffe, she recalled unwillingly, and she had seen the dog in the lane outside the house and run eagerly out of the gate to pet it. When it had turned on her snarling and bitten her hand, drawing blood, she had screamed more in terror than in pain, and Dane who was home on a short holiday had been the first to reach her. She had flung herself at him, sobbing, arms clinging, but he had put her away from him and she had been bundled unceremoniously into his car and taken to the local Cottage Hospital for the wound to be dressed, and for an antitetanus shot which had been worse. She remembered sitting beside Dane in the car, weeping, while he had said with cool contempt, 'Don't you know better than to put your hand out to a strange dog, you little fool?'

She hadn't told him that she knew very little about dogs at all. Aunt Enid had not had time for pets of any kind, and none of the neighbours in London had apparently been dog-lovers either. She had only wanted to stroke the dog, to play with him, because he had seemed friendly enough, she thought passionately. And she hated Dane more than she did already for not understanding, and for pushing her away. He was worse than the dog!

Now she smiled wryly at the memories. 'If he was treacherous, they'd hardly let him roam round loose. Besides, I've learned to deal with dogs. It's people I'm still not sure of.' As she let the Alsatian go to greet some more newcomers with a final pat, she added casually, 'Even the apparently civilised can behave like animals sometimes.'

As she stole a glance at him, she saw that her jibe had gone home. He was suddenly very pale under his tan, and his eyes were glacial, and she felt a bitter satisfaction as she walked ahead of him.

Inside the inn, she found that only the minimum concessions had been made to modernity. The ceiling still sported the original low beams and a log fire blazed brightly in an enormous stone fireplace. Solid high-backed oak settles flanked the hearth and Dane indicated they should sit there by a slight, silent gesture.

'What would you like to drink?' He fetched a menu from the bar counter and handed it to her. 'They have real ale here.'

Lisa shook her head. 'I never touch alcohol in the middle of the day. Just a tomato juice, please.'

The menu was quite short, and seemed to avoid the usual grills and basket meals, offering homely dishes like shepherd's pie and hotpot. There was also home-made vegetable soup and a selection of sandwiches.

'The soup's almost a meal in itself,' said Dane, seating himself beside her on the settle. She had hoped he would sit opposite and it was as much as she could do to stop herself edging away. 'And no doubt Chas has ordered a celebration dinner this evening.'

'For the return of the prodigal daughter,' she made her tone deliberately flippant. 'Very well, then, I'll have the soup and a round of cheese sandwiches.'

'I'll have the same,' Dane told the smiling girl who had come to take their order. Lisa noticed she had greeted him as if she knew him well, as had the landlord's wife who was serving behind the bar.

She sipped her tomato juice, and tried to ignore the curious glances coming her way, as other people in the bar half-recognised and tried to place her. But not all the glances were for her. Most of the women were looking at

Dane, some covertly, and some quite openly. There was little to wonder at in that, of course. Women had always looked and more than looked.

Lisa had to acknowledge that if she had been a stranger, seeing him for the first time, she would probably have looked herself. He was incredibly attractive, with an implicit sexuality, and the aura of unquestioned money and success to add an extra spice. And he had charm when he chose to exert it. The young waitress was clearly under his spell, but then, Lisa thought, she had never had the misfortune to cross him in any way. She would have no idea of the strength of that relentless cruelty and arrogant maleness which dwelt just below the surface glamour.

'Dane's a good friend,' she had once heard Chas telling a business associate, 'but he makes a bad enemy.'

Well, she had first-hand knowledge of just how bad that enemy could become, and it had nearly destroyed her.

Dane said, 'I hope I didn't make you cut short an important conversation back at the flat?'

After a few seconds of incomprehension, she realised he was referring to Simon's call, and she flushed a little. 'Not particularly. We'd already said what needed saying before you came back.'

'It was a man.' It was a statement rather than a question.

'It was.' He had overheard too much for her to deny it.

'*The* man?' He picked up his glass and drank from it.

'One of them.' And that had been an invention which could well backfire on her, she thought vexedly.

'You don't bestow your favours exclusively?' It was said lightly, but she could feel the undercurrent of contempt. But why should she care? She didn't want or need his good opinion.

'I'm not actually expected to.' And that at least was the truth. 'Is there any purpose behind this inquisition?'

'Naturally.' He gave her a long hard look. 'I'd like to point out that during your absence, my sister has managed to achieve a measure of stability in her life. I wouldn't want anything to upset that.'

Lisa was very still. 'I don't think I have that measure of influence over Julie.'

'And I think you underestimate yourself,' he said.

'In that case I'm amazed you should have pressed me to come back with you. I'd have thought you'd have done your utmost to ensure that I stayed away permanently.'

'If it had been left to me alone, I probably would have done,' he said levelly. 'Believe me, Lisa, the last thing I wanted was for you to come back into her life—into any of our lives, and I give you credit for equal reluctance.'

'Well, thank you.' She made no attempt to disguise the sarcasm in her voice.

'I did my damnedest to dissuade Julie from writing to you,' he went on. 'But when she enlisted Chas on her side— told him that she was writing, that she needed you, couldn't manage without you—I was left with little room to manoeuvre.'

'Unusual for you,' she said lightly. 'You're quite right, of course, I'd have kept any distance necessary to avoid having to see you or speak to you again. But I won't upset any apple carts. I'll do whatever it is Julie wants of me, and then get back to my own life.'

'That's very reassuring,' he said grimly. 'But what about Chas?'

She shrugged a little. 'I—I'll have to think of some story that will satisfy him.' She paused. 'Perhaps I should seek some assurances of my own. There must have been— speculation as to why I've stayed away all this time. May I know what you've said, if anything?'

'As little as possible, and certainly nothing approaching the truth. Did you imagine I would? Oddly enough, I prefer Chas to have some illusions left about the pair of us. Is there anything else you wanted to know?'

'Nothing,' she said, but her heart was pounding. The way he spoke, no one would credit that they had parted in violence and bitterness. She was almost glad that the waitress arrived at that moment, bringing their soup accompanied by a basket of home-made bread cut into chunks.

Lisa picked up a spoon and forced herself to begin eating. If she could maintain a cool façade, that might be her saving grace. But as she swallowed the hot savoury liquid, an instinctive pleasure in good food began to take over and she began imperceptibly to relax. If it hadn't been for the inimical presence of the man at her side, and the undoubted problems awaiting her in Yorkshire, she might even have been able to enjoy herself.

After a pause, she said, 'Is Mrs Arkwright still reigning supreme at Stoniscliffe?'

'If you want to put it like that.' He offered her the dish of sandwiches. 'You never did like her, did you, Lisa?'

She shrugged again. 'Not a great deal, but then she always made it plain she had very little time for me—or my mother,' she added.

Dane's face tightened for a moment, then he said, 'You have to remember she's been with our family a long time.'

'I'm not likely to be allowed to forget it,' she said wryly. Looking back, she could remember how difficult Jennifer's first months as mistress of Stoniscliffe had been. At first she had been difficult about making changes, a little unnerved by Mrs Arkwright's usual response to any suggestion—'The mistress always liked it done this way,' delivered in a flat tone which brooked no argument. But gradually as she gained confidence and realised that she had Chas's backing, Jennifer had quietly but firmly taken over and Mrs Arkwright had been forced to retreat, grumbling. But Lisa with a child's sensitivity had been aware that she had never forgiven or forgotten that she had been replaced as the virtual mistress of the house by someone she regarded as an interloper. As a small girl, Lisa had been made to suffer in various ways, but she wasn't the only one. Mrs Arkwright hadn't cared for Julie either and considered children generally to be an obstacle to the smooth running of any house.

In fact, Lisa had since wondered whether Mrs Arkwright's unthinking harshness in many small matters—making Julie sleep in the dark when she was frightened was only one instance—had been responsible for her stepsister's acute nervousness. All during adolescence, Julie had been subject to attacks of excitability rising at times almost to hysteria, while at school her wild and often rebellious behaviour had caused constant trouble. Persuasion worked with her most of the time, but attempts to exert any kind of authority over her caused an intense reaction. The only person she had ever seemed to be in awe of was Dane, Lisa recalled ruefully, but she knew that even he had been worried by Julie's extremes of behaviour, and had always tended to make concessions where she was concerned.

Presumably Lisa's return to Stoniscliffe had been one of these concessions, especially if Julie had exhibited any signs of becoming hysterical, and it was a weapon she had never hesitated to use whenever it had seemed likely she might be thwarted.

She sighed inwardly, wondering whether Tony Bainbridge realised just what he was taking on, or had he discovered some magic formula to control Julie by. Love could and did work miracles, of course, and yet . . .

She was suddenly aware that Dane was studying her face, his dark brows drawn together in a frown.

She said, 'I'm sorry—did you say something? I was thinking.'

'You were lost in thought.' His voice was dry. 'And not

particularly pleasant thought by all appearances.' He paused as if waiting for her to offer some explanation, and when she said nothing, he continued, 'I was merely asking whether you'd like some coffee.'

'Yes, I would.' She finished her last sandwich and sat back with a little sigh of repletion. 'That was delicious. What a lovely place this is, and the rest of the village looks interesting too. It would be nice to stay here.'

He said coolly, 'I daresay it could be arranged. It's out of season. They would no doubt have a room.'

Her eyes met his, widening in frank disbelief while the hot blood surged into her face.

She said, her voice shaking, 'I was making conversation, not issuing an invitation. Perhaps I should have made that clear.'

'Perhaps you should,' he said. His eyes slid over her cynically. 'You may be a tramp, Lisa, but you're still a beautiful and desirable woman. And you said earlier that no one had exclusive rights to you. Do you really blame me for trying?'

Anger was threatening to choke her, but she forced herself to speak calmly. 'Blame—no. Despise—yes. And now can we change the subject? I find the current one distasteful.'

'Thus speaks the vestal virgin,' he drawled. 'Only we both know how far from the truth that is—don't we, Lisa?'

For a long moment his eyes held hers, and her rounded breasts rose and fell under the force of her quickened breathing, while her small hands clenched into impotent fists.

Then she said unevenly, 'Can we go now, please? I don't think I want any coffee after all.'

'Just as you wish,' he said, and signalled for the bill. Lisa made an excuse and fled to the powder room. For a long time she stood, her fingers gripping the porcelain edge of the vanity unit, staring at her reflection with unseeing eyes.

Just what had she invited by agreeing to return to Stoniscliffe? she asked herself despairingly. She must have been insane to agree.

She ran the cold tap, splashing drops of water on to her face and wrists, making herself breathe deeply to regain her self-control. She hated him, she thought. She loathed him. She had nothing but contempt for him. So why when he had looked at her, his eyes lingering on her mouth, her breasts, had there been that small stirring of excitement deep within her, that tiny flicker of something which could only be desire?

She felt sick with self-betrayal. The poise she had so painfully acquired over the past two years seemed to have deserted her, but then Dane had always had the power to bring her confidence crashing in ruins about her. Yet it was imperative that she give no sign of this. Somehow she had to convince both Dane and herself that the most she felt for him was indifference, and that not even his most barbed remarks could hurt her any more.

It would be hard, but it had to be done. Either that or she would have to run away again, and she couldn't run for ever.

She drew a long quivering breath and went slowly back to the bar. Dane was standing talking to the landlord's wife. He was smiling, and as she looked at him Lisa was again reluctantly aware of the tug of his attraction. No woman could be proof against it, she thought. And yet she had to be. Because she could never, never let herself forget that two years ago Dane had violated her, body and soul.

It began to rain just south of Doncaster, big icy drops which battered against the windscreen with more than a hint of sleet. It seemed like an omen. Lisa thought, looking out of her window at the lowering skies, but she was only being fanciful.

They had travelled for the most part in silence. Dane had addressed a few brief remarks to her, usually connected with her comfort. Was she warm enough? Did she want the radio on? After a while, Lisa had pretended to doze. It was easier than sitting rigidly beside him, fighting to think of something to say which would not evoke any disturbing memories, or re-open any old wounds. Not that Dane had ever felt wounded, she thought bitterly.

She would be glad to get to the house now. The car she was travelling in was the last word in comfort, but she felt cramped and cooped up. A cage however luxurious was still a cage, she thought, and she had to share hers with a predator.

Once off the motorway she began in spite of herself to take more interest in her surroundings, to look about her for long-remembered landmarks. So many place names on the signposts struck answering chords within her, and most of them had happy associations—Wetherby with its race track where Chas had called her his mascot because she'd picked three winners for him on the card—Harrogate where she and Julie had been at school—York with its gated walls and towering Minster, and the little winding streets which seemed like a step into the past. She hadn't realised until that moment just how much she had missed it all, and a wave of pure nostalgia washed over her. She had been homesick, but she had managed to keep it at bay by reminding herself how impossible it was that she should ever go back.

Yet now she was back, brought by the man who had driven her into flight in the first place. And again she thought, 'I must be insane.'

The motorway was far behind them now, and it was getting dark, too dark to gain more than a fleeting impression of the surrounding countryside, the dale where Stoniscliffe was situated.

But she could remember it, could imagine the sweep of the moor, the tall rocks which pressed down to the very verges of the road, the splashing waterfalls, the march of the dry-stone walls, and the sturdy grey houses set firm against all the wind and weather could do to them.

She could gauge almost to the moment when Dane would slow for the turning which led downhill into the village. When they had been children she and Julie had always closed their eyes at that moment and counted to fifteen not too quickly, because that was how long it took to reach Stoniscliffe. Instinctively she closed her eyes and began to count, feeling the car turn in at the gate, the scrunch of the tyres over the gravel with the old familiar rush of excitement.

Dane said drily, 'You can open your eyes now. We're here.'

She obeyed, only to be almost dazzled by the lights streaming from the ground floor. The front door stood wide open, and she could see Julie's slim figure almost dancing with excitement.

Once again she had to wait impatiently for Dane to release the door catch for her, and then she was running up the three shallow steps which led to the door, and Julie was hugging her.

'Oh, Lisa—*Lisa*! It's wonderful to see you again. You wretch, to go off like that without a word to me. I have missed you so!'

She put her arm through Lisa's and took her into the house. Mrs Arkwright was waiting in the hall, neat in her dark blue dress, her grey hair arranged in its usual formal bun. Her expression betrayed neither welcome nor resentment, and Lisa looked back at her equally calmly.

'Good evening, Mrs Arkwright.'

'Good evening, miss,' the housekeeper returned. 'If you'd like to follow me, I'll show you your room.'

'There's no need for that,' Julie broke in impatiently.

'She knows which room is hers. This is her home, remember. Besides, Daddy wants to see her right away. He's been on tenterhooks ever since lunch, poor darling.' She added to Lisa in an undertone, 'Did Dane tell you about Daddy—about the wheelchair?'

'Yes, he did.' Lisa sighed. 'Why didn't you write to me, Julie, tell me?'

'Because he'd have had me hanged, drawn and quartered if I'd dared to do any such thing,' Julie said blithely. 'He hates people feeling sorry for him, or making concessions for him. He insists on doing as much as he can for himself. We thought he might be overdoing the independent bit at first, but the doctor said it was all right.' She drew a small breath. 'And now you're here and that makes everything perfect. We're a family again.'

'Until you get married,' Lisa said drily.

'Yes, I suppose so.' Julie gave a little uncertain laugh. 'I'd never thought of it in quite that way.'

Lisa squeezed her arm affectionately. 'Darling, are you happy?'

'Blissfully.' Julie lowered her voice dramatically. 'Tony worships the ground I walk on.'

'Clearly an ideal husband,' Lisa teased. 'I hope this devotion is fully reciprocated.'

'Naturally,' Julie said lightly, 'or I shouldn't be marrying him.'

She led Lisa across the hall to the drawing room door which she threw open with a flourish.

'Here she is, Daddy,' she announced.

Charles Riderwood wasn't in his wheelchair. He was up on his feet supporting himself with difficulty on two sticks.

He said, 'Lis, my dear lass.' And she ran to him.

When she could trust her voice, she said, 'So this is what you do the moment my back is turned.'

He said ruefully, 'It seems like it,' and smiled down at

her. He had lost a good deal of weight, she noticed, and there were lines of weariness and suffering marked in his face. He went on, 'But I was determined to welcome you on my own two feet, and not in that bloody thing.' He gave the inoffensive wheelchair a ferocious look.

'It looks very swish.' Lisa eyed it critically in turn. 'What are all those gadgets for? Aren't you going to give me a demonstration?'

Julie threw her a grateful look as Chas manoeuvred himself back into the chair.

He gave them a smug glance. 'I can manage, you see. We don't need that nurse. Why don't we send her packing?'

'Because Lisa and I aren't going to wait on you hand and foot, all hours of the day and night.' Julie bent and kissed the top of his head. 'You're abominable, Daddy, and you know it. Far from sending the poor soul away, I have to do a daily grovel to get her to stay here.'

The smug look deepened and he muttered, 'Woman's a fool.' Then he said more sharply, 'Where's Dane?'

'I'm here.' Dane strolled into the room. 'I was waiting until the reunion was over.'

'Oh?' His father gave him a quick frowning look. 'Well, now you are here I've got something to say to you—to both of you. I'm not blind, and I'm not stupid either, and I know quite well there was trouble between you before Lisa went away. I don't know what it was about, and I don't want to know. You're adults, not children, and you're entitled to your differences, if you want them. But now she's back with us again, in her home where she belongs, and I want an end to it. Whatever it was, it must be over and done with now, and I want peace between the pair of you.'

Dane said coolly, 'Then peace it shall be, if Lisa's willing.' He held out his hand, and numbly, unable to speak, Lisa let his fingers touch hers for a fleeting moment.

Chas gave an irritable grunt. 'That's a chilly sort of peace,' he derided. 'Kiss her and make up, man. Anyone would think you were strangers!'

Lisa stood as if paralysed. Above her, she saw Dane's face, graven as a mask. As he bent towards her, she closed her eyes in rejection, but she felt the cold swift brush of his lips on her cheek as if she had been branded there.

Chas said with satisfaction, 'That's better,' and beamed at them both. Lisa forced herself to smile back at him, but the muscles in her face felt stiff and unnatural, and she felt as if she was grimacing instead.

Dane said abruptly, 'I'll go and put the car away.' He left the room without looking at her.

Chas stared after him. 'Now what the devil's he at?' he demanded indignantly. 'Mrs Arkwright will be bringing in tea at any moment.'

Julie giggled. 'He looked as if a stiff whisky would be more in his line,' she said cheerfully. 'Come on, Lisa, let's pop upstairs and make sure you have everything you need before tea.'

On the way upstairs, she hissed, 'What on earth was all that about? Did you really fall out with Dane?'

Lisa shrugged. She felt as if she was waking slowly from a nightmare. 'In a way,' she said evasively.

'I know he can be a swine,' Julie admitted. 'He's made me feel like an—an insect regularly. But perhaps he's mellowed just lately, or I'm getting older. I'm not nearly as frightened of him as I used to be. Do you remember?'

'Only too well,' Lisa said drily, and Julie laughed.

'You always stuck up for me, didn't you, darling? You were never afraid of Dane. Whatever did he say to make you leave like that? What did you quarrel about?'

Lisa chose her words carefully. 'Well, I suppose you could say we quarrelled about you.'

'About me?' Julie sounded aghast. 'But that's terrible! I

hadn't the slightest idea. Oh, Lisa!'

Lisa gave her a slight hug. 'It doesn't matter, love. As your father said, it's all over now.' Or I hope it is, she thought, a sick feeling of panic gripping her. Oh, why did Chas have to say anything?

'But it does matter,' Julie persisted, throwing open the door of the room next to hers, the room Lisa had occupied ever since they had outgrown the shared room. 'You must tell me, Lisa. I have a right to know.'

Lisa hesitated, walking over to the bed and opening her dressing case. She began to remove her cosmetics and set them out on the dressing table.

She said slowly, 'It was about the parties you used to go to—that awful crowd you used to go round with. Dane seemed to—blame me.'

'That's idiotic!' Julie said indignantly, then she paused as a thought struck her and she gave Lisa a horrified look. 'You mean Dane knew about them—knew about the parties? Oh, God! But he never said anything. He never even *hinted* that he knew, not even when the police raided the Hammonds' and caught them smoking grass.' She shuddered. 'I wasn't there that night, thank the lord.'

Lisa gave her a steady look. 'But you'd been·there on other nights? In spite of everything you said?'

Julie shrugged, looking uncomfortable. 'Well—yes, but there's nothing in it, Lisa. I mean, everyone smokes at some time.'

'Do they now?' Lisa's head was beginning to ache, so she took the pins out of her hair and let it fall loose on to her shoulders. 'I never have. And I don't suppose Tony has either,' she added.

'Tony?' Julie laughed. 'Good God, he's far too much of a stick-in-the-mud! He got a parking ticket once and acted as if it was the end of the world.'

Lisa looked at her with slight unease. There had been a

note of scorn in Julie's voice then which had not been lost on her.

She said gently, 'It's not a bad thing to be law-abiding, you know, love. Not enough people are these days.'

'Yes, I know,' Julie said rather petulantly. 'But to get back to this business with you and Dane—are you telling me that Dane said my party-going was your fault?'

'Something of the sort,' Lisa hedged.

'And you had a row?'

'You could say so,' Lisa said wearily. 'Look, Julie, I'd really prefer to do as Chas suggested and—forget all about it.'

'Then I shall ask Dane.' Julie's lovely face wore its mulish expression and Lisa gazed at her in horror.

'No!' she exclaimed passionately. 'No, Julie, you mustn't. If you say one word about it to Dane—or anyone else for that matter—then I'll never forgive you. And I'll leave here and never come back as long as I live.'

Her words died breathlessly away into a long silence. Then Julie's lips pursed into a silent whistle of astonishment.

'You really mean that, don't you?' she said slowly. 'I'm sorry, darling. I won't say anything, if that's what you want. I'll never even mention it again. But don't go, Lisa. Please don't go. I need you—I really do. I couldn't bear it if you went away again now.' She turned away abruptly. 'I'll see you downstairs in a little while.' She went through into her own bedroom, closing the communicating door between them.

Lisa had been brushing her hair, but now she let the brush fall from her fingers to the carpet and just stood there, trying to regain her self-command.

Chas's little reconciliation scene downstairs had almost unnerved her, and she lifted a hand almost wonderingly to the cheek which Dane had kissed as if surprised to find it unmarked. She gave a little shudder. She was remembering only too vividly the last time his mouth had touched her skin, brutal, ravaging, conquering.

All the defences she had so carefully constructed against the past, against the violence, the agony and misery of that night were beginning to tumble about her. The shutter she had learned to close down in her mind wouldn't work any more.

She shook her head, rejecting the images which were beginning to crowd in on her. If she let them have their way, then she would have to leave here. But Julie needed her. Julie had said she couldn't bear it if she went away again.

She whispered, her voice shivering, 'But can I bear to stay?'

CHAPTER FOUR

DANE did not appear during tea, much to Lisa's relief. Even so she was too tense to do anything like justice to Mrs Arkwright's feather-light scones and lemon sponge. Chas frowned heavily over her lack of appetite, and she was aware of Julie watching her speculatively on more than one occasion.

She was dismayed to learn that a small celebration dinner in honour of her return to Stoniscliffe had been planned for that evening, but she tried to display moderate enthusiasm at least because it was evident that Julie had planned it with the best of intentions.

'Exactly who will be coming?' she asked.

'Well, Tony, of course,' Julie began, and Chas snorted derisively.

'Tony, of course,' he echoed. 'The amount of meals that young man eats here makes me wonder if he has a home of his own to go to!'

He gave Julie an affectionately teasing look as he spoke, but her answering smile was a little forced, as if this was a joke which was often made and which had begun to pall on her. She turned back to Lisa.

'And apart from Tony, I've only invited the Daltons. You remember them, don't you?'

'The Daltons?' Lisa frowned a little. 'You mean James and Celia? Good heavens, I thought they were in Africa, helping to put some emergent nation on to its feet.'

Chas gave a bark of laughter. 'So they were—until the nation began to emerge in a way that didn't appeal to Celia, when home they came.'

Julie added almost casually, 'They've bought the Hammonds' old place. James is working in Leeds for Celia's father.'

'In other words, back to square one,' Lisa commented. She noticed that Julie hadn't betrayed as much as a flicker when she spoke of the Hammonds' old house, almost as though it had no more significance for her than any other neighbour's house. And yet Lisa knew this could not be the case. She remembered that her mother had once said with some regret that Julie had an easy conscience and a convenient memory where her own misdeeds were concerned, and that this was not a healthy combination for any girl.

'Well, that isn't James' fault.' There was a sharp note in Julie's voice. 'When Celia holds the purse strings, she can dictate any terms she likes. You know that.'

Lisa shrugged. 'Exactly—which is why I'm a little surprised to find that you've invited them tonight. Celia was never your favourite person, I seem to remember. And she was certainly never mine.'

Julie gave Chas a limpid look. 'But Daddy likes her. He enjoys flirting with her—don't you, darling?'

Chas smiled placidly. 'Celia Dalton is an attractive woman who understands how such games should be played, but that's as far as I'm prepared to commit myself. As for James, he's not a bad lad and never was, but I'd have more respect for him if he stood up to Celia and her father occasionally.'

Julie laughed. 'You'd better not say so in front of Lisa! She used to have a terrific thing about James—still may have for all I know. We shall have to watch them closely this evening.'

Lisa's mouth curved reminiscently as she thought about James Dalton. He had for a while been her schoolgirl's ideal, with his fair hair and romantically aquiline features.

But his marriage to the arrogant and patronising Celia had soon cured that particular lovesickness, and their subsequent departure abroad had completed the task.

She said lightly, 'Let's say it will be interesting to see him again.'

As she spoke, she glanced up and her gaze slid past Julie to the door where Dane was standing. She had no idea how long he had been there, only that he had undoubtedly heard her last remark and whom it applied to, because his mouth had a contemptuous curl, and she felt the warm blood rush into her face as he looked at her.

Inward rage shook her. How dared he stand there, silently criticising and condemning, as if he honestly thought she might be contemplating a relationship with James, or anyone else for that matter?

She wanted to stand up and tell him so. To scream it at the top of her voice if necessary. To make it clear to him once and for all that any such relationships had invariably been soured and spoiled from the outset because of his brutality.

She could attract men, but that wasn't the problem. All too soon they got fed up with hanging around, being held at arm's length, waiting for a response which didn't exist in her.

And that's your fault, she wanted to cry, her finger pointed in accusation. Everything that was loving and giving in me, you took and stifled. Instead of warmth, you taught me shame. You did it, Dane Riderwood. You, and you alone.

But of course she said nothing. She didn't betray by as much as a flicker that she was even aware of his presence just picked up her cup and asked Julie calmly for more tea.

As she accepted her refilled cup with a word of thanks, another quick glance under her lashes revealed that he had gone again, as silently as he had come.

'Tony's parents would have been here tonight too,' Julie was saying. 'Only they'd already arranged to dine with friends. But I'm sure Mrs Bainbridge will throw one of her famous dinner parties for you while you're here, Lisa.'

'That sounds rather intimidating,' Lisa said, and Julie grimaced.

'It is. I don't really know how I'm going to live up to her. Cordon Bleu cook, president of the Women's Institute, magistrate, winner of cups for flower arranging—the list is endless.' She gave an affected little giggle. 'Tony wants me to call her Mother, but one couldn't possibly. Not Lydia Bainbridge. She's far too formidable. Can you imagine her doing anything as human as giving birth? I expect she ordered Tony and Melanie from a mail order catalogue, as she would her hardy annuals.'

'Formidable, perhaps,' Lisa said slowly, recalling the small upright figure of Julie's future mother-in-law, and the steely elegance which enveloped her. 'But she would have been a far better person to have helped you plan this wedding than me.'

Julie's frown was swift and thunderous. 'No, she wouldn't!' she exclaimed. 'I want someone of my own—someone from my family, not his. Thank heavens Melanie is in America or I'd have to have had her galumphing up the aisle behind me like a carthorse.'

'Julie!' Chas's voice was remonstrative. 'That's most unfair. Melanie's a nice girl, and she's no bigger than either you or Lisa.'

'Size has nothing to do with it,' Julie said rebelliously.

Lisa intervened hastily. 'Just how far have these wedding plans got?' she asked, her brow creasing. 'Wouldn't it have been better to have had it at Easter? It would have given us more time, and the weather would have been more reliable too.'

Julie gave a negligent shrug. 'Getting married at Easter is

a terrible cliché. And I hope it does snow. I love it, and I could have a velvet dress.'

'Well, that's one of the things we shall have to think about,' Lisa said. 'I suppose you've asked Mrs Langthwaite to make it for you? Have you chosen the material and had any fittings yet, because . . .'

'As a matter of fact I haven't.' Julie twisted her sapphire and diamond engagement ring in a little restless gesture. 'I—I don't want her to make it for me, Lisa. There's a boutique I know in Skipton. We can get a dress there.'

'But, Julie,' Lisa stared at her, 'Mrs Langthwaite dresses all the local brides. Won't she be very hurt?'

'Oh, I shouldn't think so. She always has more work on hand than she knows what to do with. She'll hardly miss me among so many.' Julie's tone was off hand, but Lisa knew instinctively that there was little point in pursuing the argument, even though she was amazed by Julie's decision. Mrs Langthwaite was famous for her wedding dresses, all of which were designed and made for each individual bride. Julie's plan to wear a dress bought from a shop, no matter how glamorous, would be bound to be interpreted locally as a snub, she thought ruefully.

Further questioning elicited that as the day and the time had been fixed, Julie had at least chosen and ordered the invitations.

'Not that there'll be many guests,' she added mulishly. 'I don't want my wedding turned into a public show, and if I restrict the numbers on my side, that means the Bainbridges will have to do the same.'

'I see,' Lisa said quietly. Or at least she was beginning to, she thought wryly. Julie had sent out her *cri de coeur* because she was already locked in combat with her future mother-in-law over the arrangements and wanted reinforcements in her support. It wasn't a situation that boded well for the future, and she hoped that Julie and Lydia

Bainbridge would come to terms with each other, otherwise life would be made very difficult for Tony who loved them both.

She wanted to shake Julie and tell her forcefully that Lydia Bainbridge would be far more valuable as a friend than as an enemy, but she knew it would be useless and only increase Julie's resentment more.

'We're having the reception here,' Julie continued. 'But there's no problem about that because I've booked a firm of caterers from Harrogate and they're arranging everything. They've sent some sample menus, but I simply haven't had a moment to look through them yet. Daddy's organising the champagne, of course,' she added.

Lisa looked at her in some bewilderment. Julie spoke as casually as if she was planning any ordinary party instead of her own wedding reception which was to crown what should be the happiest day of her life.

She tried to make her own tone encouraging and interested.

'Well, tomorrow we'll draw up some lists and see what still has to be done. I think studying those menus is a priority, don't you? And your dress. Once that's chosen we'll have a better idea of the sort of thing that I should wear.'

'You could wear a sack and look beautiful,' Julie said. 'Now there's a novel idea. If Melanie had been here, you could have both worn sacks and Melanie could have put hers over her head.'

'Now that's enough,' said Chas with sudden quelling authority. 'The girl is Tony's sister after all, and should have some claim on your affection because of him. So spare us the spiteful remarks, young woman.'

'Yes, Papa,' Julie said with exaggerated meekness, and Chas shook his head at her in mock exasperation.

'Have you told Lisa about the flat?' he enquired.

'Oh—no, not yet,' Julie said offhandedly.

'Flat?' Lisa queried. 'Does that mean you've found somewhere to live?'

'Oh, I didn't have anything to do with it, but—yes, we do have somewhere. There's a big disused stable block at the rear of the Bainbridges' farmhouse. Mr Bainbridge is converting it—well, he's been doing so for months, but when Tony and I decided we were getting married his parents immediately offered it to us. It was an offer we couldn't refuse.'

'How marvellous!' Lisa tried to infuse into her tone some of the enthusiasm that was definitely lacking from Julie's. 'Aren't you thrilled?'

'Naturally,' Julie said. 'Particularly by the fact that I won't actually have to live at the farmhouse, which seemed the only alternative. It's going to be beautiful, of course, with no expense spared. Tony and I are really incredibly lucky.' She gave Lisa a brilliant smile. 'You will do my make-up for the Great Day, won't you, Lisa? Is that the Amber stuff you're wearing? It's absolutely beautiful. I adore their perfume. Every time I go into Schofields, I ask the girl to spray me from their tester.' She giggled. 'One day she's going to get wise to me, and I shall actually have to buy some.'

'No need to go to those lengths,' Lisa said drily. 'I have a spare bottle you can have.'

She would have liked to have asked more about the flat, but it was clear that Julie wanted the subject changed.

When tea was over, Lisa went up to her room, pleading weariness. She was physically tired, and it was pleasant to kick off her shoes and lie down on top of her bed, but her mind was too restlessly active to allow her to relax.

She was troubled by the undercurrents that she had sensed downstairs from Julie's attitude. There was obviously something wrong, and she could only hope that it was a bad case of bridal nerves and nothing more.

At the same time she was thankful that Julie and Chas as well did not share her sensitivity, because she knew she wasn't nearly a good enough actress to pretend that all was well and normal between Dane and herself over the next weeks. She would have to try and make her avoidance of him not too obvious, of course, because the last thing she wanted was for Chas in particular to notice that there was something wrong and to be upset by it. She supposed the most she could hope for was a kind of armed neutrality, and the prospect disturbed her.

She dozed lightly and fitfully until it was time for her to have her bath and start dressing for dinner. She had deliberately brought fewer clothes than she would normally have done in order to emphasise to herself and anyone else who was interested that she had no intention of staying for any length of time. But she had included a silky jersey dress in an attractive shade of topaz, long-sleeved and with a deeply slashed vee neckline. On an impulse she brushed her hair out to hang in loose silken waves on her shoulders, and added a pair of her favourite tiger's eye studs to the lobes of her ears, and a matching dress ring for the third finger of her right hand.

She was satisfied with her appearance as she gave herself a last long critical appraisal in front of the mirror before making her way downstairs. She was the Amber Girl come to life again, and that was as good a façade as any to shelter behind.

None of the people waiting downstairs would recognise in her the rather shy schoolgirl that most of them had known her as. She took the few long, deep breaths she usually practised before she went in front of the camera and then walked out of the room and downstairs to the drawing room.

The room was lit by lamps, and a roaring log fire was

banked up on the wide hearth. Lisa stood in the doorway for a moment, looking around. James Dalton she
recognised instantly, as blond and as fine drawn as ever.
Dress him in the clothes of a bygone era instead of the
conservative dark suit he was actually wearing, and he
would be the archetype of a Romantic poet, she thought,
suppressing a faint smile. On the other hand, Tony Bainbridge, who was chatting to him, looked just what he was, a
prosperous landowner and farmer without a poetic bone in
his body. He looked sleek and well fed, whereas James had a
lean and hungry appearance.

Celia Dalton was occupying the sofa, chatting to Chas
with great admiration. She looked elegant and expensive,
Lisa thought, and as fragile as a Dresden figurine, an
appearance that was totally deceptive. Of all the people in
the room, Celia would be the last one to break.

At that moment, Chas looked up and saw her. 'Ah,
Lisa, my dear! Come in, come in. You know everyone, of
course. Celia—you remember my stepdaughter?'

'Oh, yes.' Celia glanced up with seeming casualness, but
actually missing nothing. It was the sort of look that would
have made most women instantly check their tights for
ladders, but Lisa took it in her smiling stride as she came
forward. 'Of course, you're quite a celebrity now.'

She made it sound faintly disreputable, Lisa thought
wryly, but then for Celia it probably was. In Celia's world,
you only appeared in magazines, sitting on the stairs at
hunt balls, or in newspapers, in the Birthday Honours list.

'She's more than that,' James put in, surveying her with
undisguised admiration. 'Why didn't you warn us, Lisa,
that you were going to turn into such a beauty?'

Lisa laughed, too accustomed to such remarks to be
either flattered or embarrassed by them. 'Perhaps I didn't
know myself—or better still, I wanted to surprise you all.
Hello, James—Tony. It's good to see you again.'

'It's more than good to see you,' Tony said frankly. 'As a sort of brother-in-law, do I get a kiss?'

He aimed for her lips, but by turning her head slightly, Lisa offered him her cheek with a smiling grace which robbed the action of any offence.

Dane said, 'What can I get you to drink?'

She hadn't looked for him. She hadn't betrayed the least awareness of his presence, but she had known all the same that he was there from the moment she had stood in the doorway. Even when she had been quite young, she had this ability to pick him up on some kind of invisible antennae. Perhaps it was always like this when you hated someone, she thought. Perhaps the force of your emotion made you ultra-sensitive to their presence, and their absences.

She asked for a dry sherry, her voice light and casual, and he brought it to her. She took the glass by the stem, avoiding the most fleeting contact with him, and saw his mouth twist a little as though he knew her intention. His antennae were presumably working too, she thought as she sipped her sherry and told Celia smilingly that yes, it was incredibly exciting being a model but also very hard work.

Even though the party was all her own idea, Julie came down late. Her apologies were made with a smile, but perfunctory, as if it was quite usual for the daughter of the house to be the last to arrive. She made an eye-catching picture in a dress the colour of ripe cherries, but she was wearing rather too much make-up, Lisa's expert eye noticed.

Dinner was excellent in its usual understated way—clear soup, followed by sole in a creamy sauce, and then rare roast beef with golden baked potatoes.

But no one, with the possible exception of Chas and Celia, did it justice, Lisa thought. Tony, of course, was far too busy, trying to talk to Julie whose attention like some brilliant dragonfly swooped restlessly from one to another at the dining table. James who had been placed next to

Lisa only picked at the food on his plate, so perhaps his lean and hungry look was for real, she thought drily. He chatted to her charmingly on a number of topics, but Lisa had the impression that the real James was elsewhere, hidden perhaps in some secret part of himself and quite inaccessible. She thought she remembered a warmer, more outgoing personality, but perhaps the new James represented what several years of marriage to Celia could do.

Nothing that Celia had said or done during dinner or earlier in the drawing room had gone anywhere towards reducing the animosity she had always aroused in Lisa, and yet Lisa would have been hard put to it to explain even to herself exactly why Celia made her feel as she did. In her early days in modelling she had encountered more malice and cattiness than Celia had ever displayed at her worst. At school she had met bigger snobs and far more spoiled rich girls. Usually, she could be tolerant, yet Celia had always managed to catch her on the raw.

Until now, she had always believed Julie had shared her feelings, or even exceeded them. In her younger days she had been downright rude to Celia on several occasions when the older girl had been more than usually patronising. Yet this evening Julie had been almost gushing, raving about Celia's dress, admiring what was, apparently, a new hairstyle.

Curiouser and curiouser, thought Lisa, hoping that Julie would display similar tact when dealing with her new family, but somehow doubting it.

When the three of them had returned to the drawing room when the meal was over and were waiting for coffee to be brought in, Celia said, 'Have you decided where you're spending your honeymoon yet?'

Julie gave a faint shrug. 'We've discussed it. We haven't made any firm decision.'

Celia gave the gurgle of laughter which Lisa had always loathed.

'Well, a bed's a bed no matter where you are, darling. Anyway, honeymoons are terribly overrated. I know mine was. We went to Nassau and James got food poisoning rather typically.' She shrugged. 'So I went ahead and had a marvellous time water-skiing.'

'It must have been very enjoyable,' Lisa said drily.

Celia's pale blue eyes flicked over her. 'Well, there was little point in both of us being miserable.' She turned to Julie. 'So make sure, darling, that you find somewhere where you can be entertained even if the bridegroom turns out to be a washout.' It was said with a smile, but with an underlying sting in the words, as if Celia was indicating that she expected Tony to be a blundering, insensitive disappointment to his young wife, and Lisa waited for Julie to leap to his defence.

But Julie remained silent, although Lisa saw two bright spots of colour that had nothing to do with the blusher she had applied had appeared in her cheeks, and that her eyes were stormily brilliant.

Lisa got to her feet. 'Shall we have some music?' she asked hastily, moving towards the tall antique cabinet which housed the hi-fi unit and records.

'If you wish.' Celia leaned back against the sofa cushions.

'Any requests?' Lisa began to look through the racks of records.

'Anything but Mendelssohn,' Celia murmured. 'All that dreary German romanticism . . .'

'I like Mendelssohn,' Julie said abruptly. 'Put on "Fingal's Cave", Lisa.'

'I can't seem to find it,' Lisa said mendaciously, after a pause. 'Let's have some Ravel instead.' She set the turntable in motion and soon the room was filled with the passionately mysterious strains of 'Daphnis and Chloe'.

It was a mistake, of course, and she knew it as soon as she heard the first of those evocative chords. Her hands were suddenly damp and her teeth sank into the soft underside of her lip. She hadn't been thinking when she had made that particular selection. All she had been concerned with was trying to take some of the tension out of the atmosphere, yet she had only succeeded in transferring it to herself.

It was her record, one of the many things she had left behind when she had fled from Stoniscliffe, as she thought, for ever. It had been a seventeenth birthday present, and Dane had given it to her. She could remember her surprise and her pleasure when she had unwrapped it. Any gifts she had received from him in the past had been purely duty ones, token acknowledgements of Christmas and birthdays. This was the first time that he had seemed to deliberately choose something that he knew she wanted and that would give her pleasure. So, upon the heels of her delight had come the embarrassment of having to subdue her instinctive hostility and thank him, which she had managed with a certain amount of faltering.

He'd smiled down at her, his mouth twisting cynically. 'Don't outrage your principles, Lisa,' he had advised coolly. 'It's pure selfishness on my part. I'd rather encourage your obvious penchant for the classics than have you fall into the hands of rock like Julie.'

Julie had protested indignantly and it had all ended in laughter, but Lisa had wondered about it all for a long time afterwards. She had no idea that Dane was even aware of her preferences in music. She had always supposed his indifference to her to be total, and the realisation that he might know more about her than she thought was a disturbing one.

Altogether, she thought, it had been a strange and disturbing year. She had been moody, swinging from one emotional extreme to another, as ready to cry as she was to laugh. Chas had been understanding and tolerant, ascribing her volatility to the residue of grief still remaining after her mother's death, but Lisa knew now that it hadn't been as simple as that.

Dane's gift had sparked off something deep within her, something which she was too young and untried to acknowledge or even to recognise. All she knew was that her awareness of him had increased acutely, almost painfully. She found herself listening for the sound of his car on the drive, watching him covertly in the evening when he sat talking to Chas. When he was away on business trips as he frequently was, she felt lost and somehow afraid, as if she had been cast adrift on some uncharted emotional sea.

And when he brought his girl-friends to the house, she suffered. The days when she could join Julie in her light-hearted criticism of Dane's women were long gone, she found.

And throughout it all, she played the record he had given her until it seemed she knew every note, every cadence by heart. And when she played 'Daybreak', she felt as if the music encapsulated everything she was feeling, as if it suggested the dawning inside her of something almost too wonderful to be contemplated.

And now she sat, her nails digging into the palms of her hands, her head throbbing dizzily as she remembered what it had been like to be seventeen and falling in love with Dane Riderwood.

'Just like old times,' Chas said jovially from the doorway, as he propelled himself forward into the room.

Lisa started almost guiltily, a deep flush mantling her face as Dane walked in behind his father.

He said, '"Daybreak" in the evening? I think not.' He walked across to the hi-fi, flicked a switch and the sound faded, leaving an aching silence behind it, a silence so profound that Lisa was sure that everyone must be able to hear the slow, uneven pounding of her heart.

Then Mrs Arkwright appeared with the coffee, and Celia's light drawl began describing her father's plans to extend his works, and the moment was safely past. There was even more music, Lisa realised numbly, light innocuous background stuff with no associations for anyone.

Julie said suddenly, 'If we rolled back the carpet a little, we could dance. Shall we?'

Lisa hadn't the slightest desire to dance. She wanted to seek out the sanctuary of her room, and stay there quietly until the morning, but she knew that if she made an excuse and withdrew, then the party would begin to break up and Chas would be disappointed, to say nothing of Julie.

As soon as the necessary space had been cleared, Tony was immediately at Julie's side, his arms sliding possessively round her.

Celia gave her a little gurgle again. 'How marvellous to be in love,' she commented. She smiled rather challengingly at Dane. 'Well, darling, are you going to remind me of how it once used to be?'

Silently, Dane held out his arms and Celia went into them, lifting her arms around his neck and looking provocatively up into his eyes.

Lisa was astonished at the blatancy of her behaviour and glanced quickly at James to see how he was taking it, but he didn't even seem to have noticed that his wife was clinging to another man, and again Lisa got the impression that James had withdrawn mentally to a distance. Had he forgotten, or didn't he care that Dane and Celia had once gone around together for several months?

'James,' Julie called out suddenly, 'Lisa isn't dancing.'

Lisa flushed with mingled embarrassment and annoyance as James came towards her with an apologetic air.

'It's all right, James,' she said. 'It's been a tiring day. I'd rather sit quietly with Chas anyway.'

'Oh, don't be a spoilsport, darling.' Julie detached herself from the reluctant Tony and came over to them. 'Besides, you know you really want to dance with James. She used to have the most tremendous crush on you at one time,' she added, turning to him.

Lisa's flush deepened agonisingly, and she would have liked to have taken Julie by the shoulders and shaken her.

She said quietly, 'I really don't want to dance, thanks, and I'm sure James doesn't want to hear all the lurid details of my schoolgirl fantasies.'

'Oh, I don't know,' Celia drawled. 'He might find them quite fascinating. James has forgotten how it feels to be the answer to the maiden's prayer, haven't you, sweetie?'

'If you say so, Celia.' James's voice was weary. 'Can I get you some more coffee, Lisa? Or a brandy, perhaps.'

She refused quietly and sat down beside Chas. After a pause Chas said in an undertone, 'I swear I don't know what gets into Julie at times. She wants her ears boxing.' He gave a little sigh. 'But Tony's a good, steady chap. If anyone can settle her, he should be able to.'

Lisa said 'Yes' and wished she could have agreed with a little more conviction.

The music came to an end and another record was selected.

'We must all change partners,' Julie declared. 'Tony, you dance with Celia. And Lisa—you've got to dance this time. This is your welcome home party. You can't be a wallflower.'

'Why not?' Celia asked smilingly. 'She might enjoy the novelty of the experience. After all, no one can want to be the centre of attention all the time.' Not even Lisa. The unspoken words seemed to hover in the air.

Lisa rose to her feet reluctantly. This time she would accept James's invitation, she thought. But it wasn't James who came forward and took her hand, drawing her on to the floor. It was Dane. For a moment she stiffened uncontrollably, and then realising that Chas was watching them and smiling, she forced herself to relax.

'That's better.' His voice was low and sardonic.

She did not look up at him. Instead she stared rigidly at his shoulder as if she was trying to memorise every individual thread that had gone into the making of his elegant suit.

After a pause he said, 'And how are you enjoying the fatted calf?'

'It isn't a dish I have any real taste for,' she said between gritted teeth.

'That's unfortunate. But you know how to put on an act. You do it every day for the cameras, so you can do it for Chas.'

She said steadily, 'I'm doing it now, Dane. Didn't you know?'

He looked down at her, his lips compressed, his eyes like chips of ice. He said, 'My father commented tonight that it was just like old times. He doesn't know it, Lisa, but he was wrong. There's no way you can ever get back on to the old footing in this house. Too much has happened for that. Don't even contemplate trying.'

She lifted her chin. 'You really don't have to worry. You know why I'm here, but as soon as the wedding's over I'll be gone, and nothing Chas can say or do will persuade me to do otherwise.'

'I'm glad to hear it,' he said grimly. 'And just one other word of warning. Schoolgirl crush or not, James Dalton is a married man, and Celia doesn't relinquish any of her possessions lightly, however little she may seem to value them at times.'

'Thank you for the warning,' she said tightly. 'Does Celia regard you among those possessions—for old times' sake?'

'I don't think that's any of your business,' he said too pleasantly.

'In other words, the double standard is alive and well and living in Stoniscliffe,' she said. 'Good for you, Dane. You were always a law unto yourself, and so is Celia, so you are remarkably well suited on those grounds at least.'

Dane's face darkened with anger, but he didn't answer, and presently the music ended and she escaped from him with a feeling of utter relief.

The throbbing in her head that she had been aware of earlier was now developing into a full-scale headache, and after a while, she made an excuse to Chas and went in search of some aspirin.

It was cooler upstairs and she lingered there for a while, glad of the darkness and the comparative quiet, waiting for the tablets to begin to take effect. She knew she would have to go down again, or Chas would be sending someone to find her, and she had just reached the half-landing where the wide staircase turned when she heard Julie's voice just below her, almost hoarse with passion and longing. 'Oh, darling—God, darling—I can't wait any longer!'

Lisa halted instantly, aware that her footsteps would have been soundless on the thick carpet.

It was an embarrassing situation to be in, and she turned quietly and headed back upstairs, but at the same time she was conscious of intense relief. Julie was in love, deeply and yearningly in love. No one could have doubted her feelings who had heard that note in her voice. So she and Tony would be married—and Lisa understood now, smiling wryly, Julie's insistence on haste.

Tony must have hidden depths, she decided, to have aroused such passionate desire in her stepsister, but she was thankful for it. Julie needed the stability that love and marriage would bring, and it was really no wonder that she was displaying so little interest in the actual details of the wedding. It was the belonging that she wanted, not the little rites and ceremonies and traditions that attended upon it.

She walked into her room and closed the door behind her, then looked across the room at her mirrored reflection. She saw what anyone would see—the Amber Girl, poised and confident, the girl with the world at her feet. And watched while the image disintegrated until there was only Lisa—alone, unhappy and afraid.

CHAPTER FIVE

SHE awoke with the sensation that she was suffocating, that someone had laid a stifling hand across her mouth. It was dark, and for a moment she stared uncomprehendingly into the blackness, trying to orientate herself. Then she realised what had happened.

She had been so weary by the time she actually came to bed that she had forgotten to turn off the large radiator or open a window, with the consequence that her room was now like an oven.

With a sigh, she pushed back the bedclothes and padded barefoot across the soft carpet to the window. She dealt with the radiator first, then drew back the heavy curtain so that she could reach the window catch. Airless rooms were a small phobia of hers, and it said a great deal for her highly-charged mental state when she had come to bed that she had failed to make her usual preparations.

The catch was a little stiff, and as she struggled with it, she was suddenly aware of movement in the garden below. She stared down and saw a tall figure walking slowly, the glow of a cigar butt.

There was no reason why he should look up. He could have no reason to suppose there would be any witnesses of his vigil, yet Lisa drew back behind the curtain, her heart thumping. Seeing him down there was a shock, and yet it shouldn't have been. Going for long walks in the middle of the night, while he worked out some problem either business or personal had long been an idiosyncrasy of Dane's. In fact it had been because of that . . .

Lisa froze inwardly, trying to operate the shutter in her

mind, to blank out the crowding memories. But now they were proving too strong for her. There were too many associations to contend with—this house, the music she had played earlier, and now Dane himself pacing the garden as he had been doing that night two years ago.

Shivering, Lisa got back into bed, and lay staring at the shadows in the room. There were differences, of course. It had been summer then, for one thing, and Julie was in bed and asleep in the next room now instead of roaming heaven knew where.

Ever since they had come home from school, Julie had been causing problems, Lisa recalled. She had been behaving badly during the term and there had been confrontations with several members of staff. So she had come home loudly demanding to be sent elsewhere, swearing she wouldn't go back to school in September. But Chas was adamant. It was a good school with a fine reputation, and she was staying, he had told her, adding frostily that he expected a better report at the end of the next term than the one he had just received.

'I won't go back. I hate the place!' Julie had stormed to Lisa when they were alone. 'I'm sick of wearing that stupid uniform and being treated as if I was a kid—and a mentally deficient one at that. Bed at nine-thirty indeed!'

'It hasn't really done either of us any harm.' Lisa tried to speak pacifically, but Julie refused to be soothed.

'When we were children, perhaps. But I'm not a child, I'm a woman.'

It was a defiant claim which was to be repeated often over the next few weeks, so much so that Lisa grew to dread it. At first she didn't associate Julie's growing rebelliousness with the Hammonds. Julie had met Anthea Hammond at the local tennis club which she and Lisa both belonged to in the holidays. Although she was considerably younger than Anthea, Julie was a talented player and she

was clearly flattered when the other girl asked her if she
would like to enter the club tournament as her doubles
partner.

The Hammonds hadn't lived in the area for very long.
Mr Hammond was a wealthy industrialist, and his wife
was a designer who spent a good deal of her time in London.
Consequently their two children Laurie and Anthea had
the run of the house to themselves more often than not.
It was a big house, luxuriously furnished and standing in
splendid grounds, with its own tennis court and a heated
swimming pool. Lisa found it oppressive, but as she reminded herself, this could have been because she didn't
care for the Hammonds as a family, and felt strongly for
no very clearly defined reason that they were a bad influence on Julie.

Yet there was no way to stop Julie going there. She
went over each day to practise her tennis with Anthea, and
Lisa stifled her misgivings. Nor did she mention them to
Chas. After all, she reasoned with herself, she had no
real grounds for doing so, and anyway relations were as
near strained between Julie and her father as they were
ever likely to be, and no good could be accomplished by
creating even a minor conflict over the Hammonds.

Even when she started hearing the rumours, Lisa still
hesitated. So the Hammonds had wild parties—well, they
were both well over the legal age of consent and old enough
to drink or pursue any other stimulant which took their
fancy. At least Julie would never be at any of them;
Chas would never allow either of them to go to parties
where the parents of the host or hostess were likely to be
absent. Julie had often protested that this was stuffy, but
Chas was determined, and the rule was adhered to.

Or at least Lisa had thought it was, until one night a
slight noise had awakened her, and she had gone into
Julie's room, to find her stepsister frantically trying to

scramble out of her clothes and into her pyjamas at three in the morning. And Lisa could smell the alcohol on her breath from across the room.

'Julie, you fool!' was Lisa's immediate reaction. 'How long has this been going on?'

Julie's eyes were sullen. 'Oh, don't make a song and dance over it, Lisa,' she said angrily, slurring the words a little. 'If I'm going to be shut in that juvenile prison for three parts of the year, at least I'm going to enjoy myself for the rest of the time!'

'And this is your idea of enjoyment?' Lisa's voice was bitterly derisive. 'Slipping out of the house when everyone's asleep, betraying your father's trust, getting drunk . . .'

'I'm nowhere near bloody drunk,' Julie retorted violently. 'So stuff you, Miss Prim and Proper!'

'Thank you,' Lisa said quietly, and turned to leave.

'Lisa!' Julie flew across the room and caught her arm. 'I'm sorry—I didn't mean it. Yes, I have had a few drinks, but I'm not drunk, really I'm not. And Chas has never really objected to either of us having a drink, you know that.'

'At Christmas, and the occasional sherry or table wine on Sundays,' Lisa pointed out. 'Not spirits—ever. And nowhere other than home. You're under age, Julie. You're not even sixteen yet. What else have you been doing as well as drinking?'

'Well, not what you think.' Julie gave a little giggle and covered her mouth with her hand, while she stared at Lisa with an expression which combined insolence with an odd kind of pleading in her eyes. 'Lisa, you aren't going to tell Daddy about this, are you? You wouldn't be so mean! I just wanted a bit of amusement, and I like Anthea even if you don't. But I won't go again. I promise you I won't just as long as you don't tell Daddy.'

Lisa was torn as she looked at Julie's flushed face and

over-bright eyes. She knew that Chas ought to be told, but she also knew how upset he would be. She was also reluctant to jeopardise her close relationship with Julie who had always confided in her in the past, and this was coupled with a natural distaste for tale-bearing anyway. And Julie had given her word . . .

'All right,' she said with a sigh. 'I won't say anything to Daddy. But this had better be the last time, Julie. I don't want to know how many times you've got away with this in the past, but what you must understand is that there's no future in it. The Hammonds are a rotten pair—there's all kinds of gossip about them already, and Daddy would hit the roof if he thought you were in any way involved.' She paused, then added, 'You'd better tell Anthea to find herself another tennis partner as well.'

'No problem.' Julie's smile had an unpleasantly knowing quality which was too old for her years. 'I don't think Anthea's particularly interested in tennis any more.'

As Lisa went back to her room, she decided rather grimly that it might be better not to enquire too closely into the implications of that comment.

The trouble was the Hammonds' house was only divided from Stoniscliffe by their respective gardens and a couple of paddocks, so it had been all too easy for Julie to slip out of the house and make her way there unseen.

Well, it will just have to be made more difficult in future, Lisa told herself, even though Julie had given her word that she would not go there again.

I think that decision requires a little reinforcement, Lisa thought.

The following day she walked over to the house. Julie had spent the day in bed, complaining that she had had too much sun the day before but suffering in reality, Lisa suspected, from a hangover.

Guided by the sound of voices, she made her way round

to the side of the house where the swimming pool was situated. Laurie and Anthea Hammond were there sprawled on loungers at the side of the pool, and neither of them, Lisa was embarrassed to see, with a stitch on, although Laurie did eventually have the grace to reach for a towel and drape it round himself with a faintly derisive grin.

'Well, hello,' Anthea drawled. 'To what do we owe this honour?'

'It isn't a social call,' Lisa said bluntly, ignoring Anthea's languidly gestured invitation to sit down. 'I've come to tell you that I know Julie's been attending your parties, and that you've been encouraging her to drink and God knows what else, and I'm telling you now it has to stop, or I shall inform my stepfather, and then you'll both find yourself in more trouble than you've ever dreamed of.'

'Threats yet!' Anthea stretched like a cat and sat up, her bare limbs glinting with sun oil.

Laurie was grinning again, and his eyes ran over Lisa in insolent appraisal.

'Don't panic, tigress, you can have your cub back. She's a little too immature as yet for most tastes.' His eyes lingered hotly on the swell of Lisa's breasts beneath the thin cotton dress. 'Now, if you were to offer to take her place . . .'

'No, thank you,' Lisa said icily.

'No? Pity.' Brother and sister looked at each other and laughed. They made Lisa's flesh crawl.

'One more thing,' she made her voice brisk and authoritative. 'Please don't communicate with Julie in any way, or encourage her to come over here on any pretext.'

'You're fooling yourself, darling,' Anthea said with a sneer. 'Your innocent lamb didn't need any encouragement. It was all her own idea. We don't throw children's parties, actually. Now, you can find your own way out, I hope.'

'I can,' said Lisa, and turned away. She was halfway

across the second paddock when something made her look back, and she saw that Laurie Hammond had followed her and was standing at the gate in the dry stone wall watching her. As she hesitated, he waved to her, and lifted his hand to his lips to send her a mocking kiss. She turned back abruptly and continued on her way, resisting the impulse to run.

As she opened the gate which led into the garden and stepped through into the shrubbery, a hand fell on her arm and she stifled a scream.

'Oh, Dane!' Relief made her feel weak. 'You—you startled me.'

'So I see.' His voice sounded grim. 'Where have you been?'

She shrugged evasively. 'Just for a walk.'

'Alone?'

'Of course.'

'Don't lie to me, Lisa,' he said wearily. 'I saw your— companion's farewell from my window. It overlooks the paddock, in case you'd forgotten.'

She was about to deny vehemently any association with Laurie Hammond when the thought struck her that Dane might then reasonably ask why she had been calling at the house, and that would involve Julie, which was the last thing she wanted.

Dane's eyes were like winter as they looked at her. 'I didn't know Laurie Hammond was your type.'

She shrugged. 'In a place like Stoniscliffe there isn't a great deal of choice.' She tried to keep her voice light.

His mouth twisted with unmistakable contempt. 'I suppose not. But I'd begun to give you credit for more sense, Lisa. I'm sorry to find out that I was wrong.'

He turned and walked away, and Lisa looked after him wretchedly. She wanted so desperately to tell him the truth, but under the circumstances it was impossible.

The next three weeks passed quietly enough. The good weather broke and was followed by a period of squally rain and high winds, which made Julie fret, claiming that she was bored and that life at Stoniscliffe was as bad as being at school.

Lisa was worried by this and kept more than a careful eye on her stepsister, even opening her bedroom door hours after Julie had retired to check that she was actually in bed and asleep.

But it seemed that Julie was being as good as her word, and when Lisa learned through local gossip that the Hammonds had gone down to London to visit their mother, she was able to relax.

The return of a golden summer seemed like a good omen, she thought, and not even Chas's departure for the States on a business trip could disturb her optimistic mood.

What a fool I was, Lisa thought, tossing restlessly in her bed. What a blind, complacent fool!

The nightmare had begun quietly enough. It had been a hot, sultry day with the promise of thunder in the air. Julie had been languid, complaining of a headache, so Lisa was unsurprised when after dinner she said she would have an early night.

Lisa had remained alone in the drawing room. She had switched on the television, but none of the programmes seemed to hold any appeal for her, so she turned eventually to her favourite music.

She was so absorbed that she didn't hear the car, wasn't even aware as she sat curled up on the sofa that she was no longer alone until she glanced up and saw Dane looking down at her. He hadn't been expected until the following day, and she scrambled off the sofa with a little cry.

'Oh—you're back. Why didn't you warn us? We've had dinner, but . . .'

'It's all right.' He lifted his hand wearily. 'I'm not that

hungry. Mrs Arkwright is taking some coffee and sandwiches to the study.'

She said, 'Oh,' again. She gathered a little smile. 'Well—
if that's what you want.'

'It will do,' he said. 'I'll leave you in peace with your
music. Where's Julie?'

'She wanted an early night.' Her mouth felt suddenly dry,
and she moistened her lips with the tip of her tongue.
'You—you don't have to eat in the study, Dane. You could
have your meal in here.'

His mouth twisted slightly. 'I didn't think my company
was all that welcome.' His eyes met hers directly and a
curious little shiver ran through her body.

She said in a low voice, 'It's always been you who's avoided
me.'

'How very eccentric of me,' he said gravely. 'Shall I tell
Mrs Arkwright to bring my supper in here?'

With a fair attempt at nonchalance, she said, 'Why not?'

Dane gave her a long rather enigmatic look, then crossed
to the door and went out.

Lisa leaned back against the sofa cushions and closed her
eyes, aware that her pulses were behaving oddly. She had
been alone with Dane before many times. They lived in the
same house, and were part of the same family. But this was
different and she knew it. This time a deliberate choice had
been made and by them both.

She swallowed convulsively, feeling the wild coursing of
her blood through her veins. Then she got up and went over
to the hi-fi unit. She selected Ravel's 'Daphnis and Chloe'
and put it on the turntable.

The music seemed to surge into the room, mirroring the
emotional turmoil within her. She cleared a small table
and brought it over to the sofa. Then she sat down and
waited, her hands folded in her lap, her heart thumping
painfully.

When Dane came back, carrying a tray, she saw that he had changed out of the dark business suit into casual grey trousers and a matching rollneck sweater in thin wool.

His brows rose when he looked at the table. 'Very domestic,' he commented, and Lisa flushed.

'You're laughing at me,' she accused in a low voice.

'And that isn't allowed? Well, in view of our past relations, perhaps not.' He set down the tray. 'Coffee?'

She shook her head. She was shaking so much inside that she would be bound to spill the liquid or choke on a crumb. At any other time it wouldn't have mattered, but this evening everything seemed to have an overwhelming importance.

'You must have something.' There was a note of impatience in his voice. 'You've been losing weight.' He put out his hand and lifted her chin, studying her face as if he had never seen it before. 'What is it?'

'Nothing,' she denied hurriedly. 'I—I just haven't been sleeping too well, that's all. I think it's the hot weather.'

'Or stress.' He made no attempt to release her. 'Worried about school? Anxious about the future—or what?'

She swallowed convulsively. 'No—there's nothing.'

'I see.' He was silent for a moment, then his hand fell away and he turned away almost dismissively, pouring coffee into his cup and reaching for one of the sandwiches. 'And after all, why should you confide in me? I've never exactly encouraged you to up to now.'

Lisa said, 'No,' in a subdued tone.

'But I can at least encourage you to eat.' He held out the plate to her. 'Chicken or ham.'

She took a sandwich and forced herself to eat it, aware that he was watching her, his grey eyes cool and speculative.

When he had finished his meal he replaced his cup and plate on the tray and leaned back, closing his eyes. Lisa moved, intending to take the tray to the kitchen, but his hand shot out and captured her wrist.

'Leave those things,' he ordered. 'Just sit still and relax for a while. You look as if you're strung up on wires.'

She sank back against the cushions, biting her lip nervously. To be ordered to relax was one thing, but to obey was quite another, when every nerve ending in her body was screaming her awareness of him.

She said, babbling a little, 'Do you think there's going to be a storm? It's been threatening all day and the air feels so heavy.'

'You're not frightened of storms, are you?' Dane said lazily, his thumb making gentle stroking movements on the inside of her wrist. 'Is that why you're so tense?'

The almost casual caress was making her pulses go crazy. In the past, physical contact between them had been non-existent, so she had no means of knowing whether this would be the effect his lightest touch would always have had on her. But she doubted it. If he had ever touched her in the past, then it would have been in a brotherly way, but now the soft movement of his hand on her skin was telling her quite clearly that there was no kinship between them except that of the flesh.

He said softly, 'You're trembling, Lisa. Is it because you're worried about the storm or—is it this?'

He bent towards her and his mouth brushed across hers in a featherlight touch that made her lips feel oddly bruised.

She gasped, and her lips parted, mutely inviting the repetition of his kiss. He drew a sharp breath, staring down at her, his eyes suddenly harsh and bright, and then his mouth descended on hers with a searching intensity which drove all coherent, sane thought from her mind.

She was conscious of nothing but Dane, his hands holding her, the weight of his body pinning her against the cushions. Her response was total, unequivocal. She had hungered for him for months and not known it, or not admitted it, but now she knew, and her admission was made in a whimper of satisfaction against the hardness of his mouth.

His kiss deepened and demanded beyond the possibility of her experience. She was swimming in deep waters, caught by unknown currents, and she was content to let the floodtide of untried emotions carry her along.

She had always hated him, never trusted him, yet now he was all her senses craved, and she submitted unquestioningly to his ruthless invasion of her awakening senses.

His hands were no longer gripping her bruisingly, but moving with slow expert sensuality, moulding her against him, making every inch of her conscious of the same aching excitement. Under their thin Indian cotton covering, her breasts were full and throbbing, the nipples swollen as they pushed against the warm muscular wall of his chest.

The bodice was low and square-necked, fastened by half a dozen tiny buttons covered in the same material as the dress. Very slowly and deliberately, without fumbling, he began to unfasten the buttons. The dress fell away and Dane looked down at her, his breathing perceptibly quickening. Then he bent his head and his tongue gently teased first one delicate pink bud, and then the other.

Lisa was hardly breathing. Her eyes were wide and very brilliant, glowing with the delight of her first experience of physical enslavement.

His mouth lingered on her breasts, his lips and tongue tracing small erotic patterns on her skin, while his hands slid slowly downwards, losing themselves among the soft folds of her skirt. Dimly she was aware of the music swelling and soaring. Daybreak, she thought dazedly, the beginning of life, the dawning of joy—each and every day-break in Dane's arms.

And then like a sudden shower of cold water, she heard another sound, brisk and intrusive, the sound of Mrs

Arkwright's footsteps coming along the corridor, and the swift, sharp knock on the door.

The sweet sensual spell which seemed to bind them was broken. Dane jack-knifed away from her with a muttered curse, feverishly raking his fingers through his dishevelled hair.

He said in a savage undertone, 'Fasten your dress,' as he piled the used crockery back on to the tray. Lisa obeyed, but her shaking fingers made her clumsy, and Mrs Arkwright knocked again impatiently. At last she forced the last button back through its loop and Dane called, 'Come in.' He was standing over by the french windows looking out into the garden, holding back one of the long velvet curtains.

Mrs Arkwright came bustling in, then checked. 'I didn't know Miss Lisa was here, sir.'

Lisa felt herself flushing as she heard the disapproval in the housekeeper's voice. The fact that she and Dane were now on opposite sides of the room meant nothing. Mrs Arkwright was no fool and the rumpled sofa probably told its own story.

Dane said coolly, 'Does it matter?'

'It's just that there was a phone call for her, sir. I daresay you didn't hear the phone because of the music. I went up to her room to look for her, but had to tell the caller I thought she'd gone for a walk.'

'Who was the caller, Mrs Arkwright?' Lisa asked.

'Mr Laurence Hammond, Miss Lisa. He asked me to give you the message that the invitation stood for this evening.'

Mrs Arkwright collected the tray and departed.

'Since when have you been accepting invitations from Hammond?' Dane asked bleakly.

'I haven't,' she protested. 'I don't know what he's talking about. It must be some kind of obscure joke.'

'It seems relatively straightforward to me.' His voice

was grim. 'Apparently you have a date with him tonight, which I've been selfishly keeping you from. My apologies.'

Lisa got to her feet. 'But it just isn't true! I wouldn't go out with Laurie Hammond. I don't even like him.'

'You appeared to be on good enough terms a few weeks ago,' he said. 'Yet you're very quick to deny any association with him. Why, Lisa? Is it because you know that Chas wouldn't approve?'

Only minutes before he had been her tutor in the first intimate lessons of lovemaking, but now they were miles apart again, with all the old hostility and mistrust vibrating between them.

She said on a note of swift anger, 'No, he probably wouldn't approve, but then I don't suppose he'd be overly impressed with your behaviour of the past half hour either.'

'How very true,' he said sardonically. 'Perhaps Mrs Arkwright's interruption was more timely than I thought. Purely as a matter of interest, do you make a habit of behaving like that, because if so I advise you to be very careful, particularly where Hammond and the bunch he runs around with are concerned.'

There was a note in his voice that made something shrivel and die inside her.

She said, lifting her chin, 'Thank you for the warning, but I assure you it isn't necessary. I can take care of myself.'

Without hurrying, she turned and left the room.

She thought at first that it was the crack of thunder which had woken her. She lay still in the darkness listening to the lashing of the rain against her window. The storm had broken in earnest, she thought sleepily. It sounded as if it was hailing. The tinkling against her window wasn't like ordinary raindrops. In fact it sounded more like pebbles, as if someone was throwing handfuls of gravel . . .

She pushed back the covers and jumped out of bed. She opened the window and looked out and down into the darkness, gasping a little as the damp chill of the air rushed at her. The lightning flashed and she thought she saw the pale oval of a face looking imploringly up at her, and before the crash of the thunder a whispered entreaty, 'Lisa!'

Julie's voice, she thought frantically. But she had looked in earlier and her stepsister's bed had been occupied. She would have sworn it was.

She called down in a low voice, 'I'm coming.'

Not bothering with slippers or a dressing gown, she slipped out of the room and downstairs to the side door. It was unbolted, she noticed, but the catch had been dropped. When she opened it, Julie was huddled in the porch. She had a light raincoat huddled around her, but her hair was hanging in dripping rats' tails around her face, and her feet were bare and muddy.

Lisa gasped. 'Julie—you'll catch pneumonia!' She hauled the shivering girl into the house and gave her a little shake. 'Where on earth have you been?'

Julie looked at her piteously. 'Oh—Lisa!' She seemed about to dissolve into tears.

Lisa bit her lip. 'It's all right, I suppose I can guess. Come upstairs at once and get out of those wet things. And where are your shoes?'

'I dropped them,' Julie whispered. 'I'd taken them off so I could run faster, but I heard someone following me, and I —panicked, I suppose, and dropped them.' She gave a little shudder. 'They were my new ones, with high heels. I—I couldn't run in them, you see, and . . .'

'Never mind, love, never mind,' Lisa said gently. 'Don't talk now. Let's get you upstairs and warm and dry.'

But as she propelled Julie up the stairs, she found herself wondering in a kind of anguish what had made her stepsister run away barefoot through a storm, and felt her hands curl into claws as she thought of the Hammonds.

She was thankful that Chas was away. His room was nearer to theirs and he might well have been disturbed by the noise, because Julie was crying openly now, a low monotonous sobbing.

Lisa hustled her into her own room and got her out of her wet clothes and into a dressing gown, while she ran a hot tub in the adjoining bathroom. She filled a hot water bottle while she was about it and took it into Julie's room, re-coiling with a little cry when she saw the motionless shape in the bed.

Julie said from the doorway, 'I used some of the spare pillows from the linen cupboard. I knew you used to look in each night, and that you'd come looking for me if you knew the bed was empty.'

Lisa pulled back the covers and tossed the pillows on to the floor. 'Clever,' she commented shortly. 'How many times have you played this little trick?'

'This was the first.' Julie's face crumpled a little. 'I know you won't believe me, but . . .'

'Why should I believe you? You gave me your word, and you broke it.' Lisa put the bottle in the bed and tucked the covers around it.

'I didn't mean to.' Julie shrugged wearily. 'I was just so—bored. And when Mrs Arkwright came up and knocked on the door and called out that Laurie had been phoning you, I just decided I'd go over there.' She shivered. 'But I never will again. It was horrible! They had a lot of people there I'd never met before—not the usual crowd, older people. I didn't like them. They said we were going to play games, and I asked what sort of games because they seemed—well, too old really, and they laughed and said party games, and that I'd enjoy them.' She put her hand over her mouth and closed her eyes. 'It was a kind of Forfeits,' she said in a muffled voice. 'And when I realised what they were going to do—what they wanted me to do, I got scared and I ran away, and Laurie came after me. He'd been drinking, and he said horrible things to me—about me being a gate-crasher and a silly little prude, and that I'd have to pay the first forfeit because I hadn't been invited.' She stopped and looked at Lisa, her eyes very wide. 'I ran,' she said.

Lisa felt nauseated, but she smiled gaily and encouragingly.

'Of course you did, love.' Her voice was soothing. 'And now it's all over and you'll never have to see any of them again.'

She got Julie into the warm water and made her relax and later helped her get dry as if she had been a small child again, and into her pyjamas. Julie looked very small against her pillows, and very flushed, her eyes filling with that hysterical brightness, Lisa noted with a sinking heart.

She said, 'Try to get some rest, darling. It's nearly dawn, you know. I'll leave my door open and you can call me if you want anything.'

'I do want something.' Julie's hand clutched at hers feverishly. 'I want my shoes, Lisa. Please—you must go and get my shoes!'

'Of course I will. I'll get them tomorrow.'

'No, now. Please go now.' Julie's head began to thresh around on the pillow. 'If you leave them until tomorrow someone else might find them. Someone might bring them here and Dane would find out and he'd tell Daddy. Please, Lisa, please get them for me!'

Lisa detached herself gently. She was frowning a little. The storm had passed over, and the rain seemed to have stopped, but the prospect of going out into the wet darkness to search for a pair of dropped shoes was not one that had the slightest appeal. Julie was being thoroughly unreasonable, but then when she worked herself up into one of her hysterical states, there was no reasoning with her, as

Lisa knew only too well.

She said reluctantly, 'All right, love, I'll go now.'

She went back to her own room and put on the dress she had been wearing earlier and a pair of thonged sandals on her bare feet. She found a torch and put Julie's still damp raincoat round her shoulders before venturing downstairs again.

This time, to her surprise, the side door was not only shut but bolted, and Lisa knew this was not her doing. She had been too concerned to get Julie upstairs to bother much with security. She drew back the bolts carefully and went out leaving the door unlatched. She would make a token search, she told herself, and have a proper hunt for the shoes in daylight.

But as it was, she found them without too much difficulty, just beyond the gate which led from their paddock into the shrubbery. Lisa shook the surplus water from them, then tucked them into the pockets of the raincoat and started to walk back to the house. She let herself in quietly, re-locked and bolted the side door and put the raincoat and shoes in the downstairs cloakroom before wearily climbing the stairs.

She had only taken two steps along the gallery leading back to her room when a hand fell on her shoulder.

Dane said bitingly, 'Welcome home.'

He was very angry, she realised at once, but commingled with the anger there was some other element, some other emotion she could not so easily analyse, but it disturbed her and she tried to back away, but his grip tightened until she winced.

He was wearing a towelling bathrobe, and nothing else as far as she could judge, and his hair was wet as if he had just been taking a shower.

He said slowly, 'I wondered when I found the side door unbolted, but I thought perhaps Mrs Arkwright might have slipped up for once. I suppose I should have realised—after that phone call this evening. Did you enjoy the party, Lisa? Rumour has it that they're quite something, but all the same I didn't think that you—even you wouldn't stoop so low.'

She wanted to deny it, to scream her denial at him, but the bitter contemptuous words 'even you' held her silent. Nothing had changed, she thought wretchedly.

She had lain awake for hours thinking about Dane, and about his lovemaking, wondering and hoping, asking herself what difference it would have made if they had not been interrupted at that particular moment. He had desired her. He had shown her so with the utmost frankness, but there had been tenderness too, or so she had thought . . .

Looking at him now, though, it was impossible to believe that he had even been capable of such emotion. There was no gentleness about him now. Just a cold bitterness which was almost tangible and made the summer dawn dark.

'Trying to think of a convincing story?' His voice went on remorselessly. 'Forget it, Lisa. I can see the paddock from my window, if you remember, and I saw your torchlight bobbing about. Why didn't you stay the night—or has your lover got tired of you already?'

She felt every word as if it was a blow, and she was reeling under them.

She said, 'I have no lover.'

'No?' His mouth curled. 'Amazing—because you're not exactly unwilling, are you, sweetness? You don't even like me, and yet I could have had you earlier tonight. And do you know what stopped me—apart from Mary Arkwright's sudden appearance? I thought you were innocent —that you didn't really know what you were doing. And I didn't want to damage that innocence.' He gave a swift

savage laugh. 'God, what a fool—what a blind, stupid fool!
I couldn't sleep tonight, so I went walking. All I could see
was your face, your body. I was like a starving man watching
a banquet from a distance. And all the time you were with
that scum, letting him make a meal of you.'

He was gripping her by both shoulders now. Lisa thought
her very bones would be bruised, but she wouldn't let
herself cry out.

She said, 'I can take care of myself.'

His voice softened, but there was a note in it which made
her blood run cold.

'I'm sure you can. So let's begin again, shall we, Lisa,
my lovely Lisa with the limpid innocent eyes? Only we
won't bother with the innocence this time. Let's see what
other tricks you have in your repertoire.'

She protested on a little moan of sheer terror, 'Dane—no!
It isn't what you think. Really . . .'

He laughed jeeringly. 'No? But then it never has been
what I thought. So we won't bother thinking—either of us,
sweetness. We have enough going for us without that.'

He jerked her forward, his mouth suddenly brutally
possessive on hers. She began to struggle, her hands
beating against the hard wall of his chest, but to no avail.

When he released her his breathing was uneven and his
eyes glittered. He said thickly, 'What are you wearing
under that dress—anything? How very convenient. I don't
think I'll bother with those bloody little buttons this
time.

He wrenched at the neckline and it tore like paper.
Lisa gave a little agonised cry and tried to snatch at the
material, to hold it against her, but Dane was too strong, too
determined.

He said on a snarl, 'Don't look so stricken, my lovely
one. You've let other people see you like this—kiss you—
touch you. Now it's my turn.'

He picked her up in his arms and carried her to his room, kicking the door shut behind them. She was struggling like a wild thing, biting and scratching, but he didn't even seem to notice.

As he threw her across the bed, she sobbed out, 'Dane—no! Please—no!'

His mocking smile made him look like a devil as he tossed the dressing gown aside and bent over her. 'Yes, Lisa, please, yes.' His voice altered and roughened. 'Sluts don't have a choice, darling. And you've forfeited yours.'

Forfeits, she thought wildly. Julie had been talking about forfeits. She'd been frightened, and she'd run away. Lisa was frightened too, more frightened than she had ever been in her life, only there was nowhere to run to.

Somewhere there were birds singing, acclaiming the birth of the new day. She had dreamed of a dawn and Dane's arms round her—only not like this—never like this. This was a nightmare.

He said harshly, 'Relax, damn you, or you're going to get hurt.'

She was hurt already. She had never imagined such pain, such bitterness of mind and body. She buried her teeth in her lower lip to prevent herself from whimpering. Outside, in the western sky, there would be pale streaks of light, but inside the room there was darkness, only darkness, and it rose up around her, engulfing her, and she slid submissively into its depths.

CHAPTER SIX

LISA sat bolt upright in bed, both hands pressed against her mouth. She was shaking like a leaf. This was what she had been afraid of. This was why she had not wanted to come back to this house. Because she had always known that if she did come back she would have to think about what had happened, to remember every detail.

For two years, she had been able to pretend, to block it out of her mind, but now she had no reserves of pretence to fall back on. She had to remember everything.

Afterwards, when it was over, she had lain there quietly beside Dane, waiting, hoping that he would fall asleep. At last she had moved, softly, tentatively easing her aching body towards the edge of the bed, away from him, only to hear him laugh softly in the darkness.

'Tired of me already?' he'd jibed. 'Don't I turn you on like Hammond does? Well, you were rather a disappointment yourself, sweetness. Where's all the passion you let me taste earlier?'

'I hate you,' she'd whispered. 'God, how I hate you!'

She had felt rather than seen him shrug. 'Hate me all you want,' he said coldly. 'But you're not leaving. I haven't finished with you yet, Lisa.' His hand cupped her breast, then slid downwards, exploring the swell of her hip. He said, 'You wanted me earlier tonight, and you'll want me again. It's as simple as that, Lisa. It has nothing to do with love or hate, or even right or wrong. It's purely chemistry.' He bent his head, brushing his lips softly across the tautened peaks of her breasts. 'Let me show you.'

'No!' She had stiffened in rejection and alarm, trying to

94

push away the hand which was gentling her as if she was a frightened animal.

'Hush,' he said. He kissed her mouth, but with none of the earlier brutality, parting her lips sensuously, caressing the flesh with intimate gentleness. 'Don't fight me, Lisa.' His voice deepened, roughened slightly. 'Don't fight yourself.'

With bewildered shame she had known he was right. That it was only her stubborn, bruised mind that was still resisting. He had taken her without gentleness, without respect for an innocence he was still not prepared to acknowledge, yet in spite of his ruthlessness he had awakened some dormant spark, set new fire to her inborn yearning for fulfilment.

He had used her quite cynically for his own gratification, but her instinct told her that next time—this time it would not be like that.

Only there would not be a next time, Lisa thought, shutting her ears to the clamouring of her senses. She would not accompany him down this dark, mindless path to pleasure. She would not deliver herself body and soul into his thrall. If she didn't fight him now, then her surrender would be unconditional. She knew that. He had the power to make her his slave, his thing.

Oh God, she thought, the bitterness rising in her throat. Didn't he despise her enough already? She had to get away from him, away from Stoniscliffe, before he guessed how complete his savage victory had been.

She looked up at him, into the dark face that was studying hers with such intentness, as if he was trying to read the thoughts behind her shuttered eyes, and she smiled, her lips curving in derisive amusement.

She even managed a little rueful laugh. 'Sorry, Dane. I'm sure you meant it to be terribly punitive and instructive—and it was, but that's all it was.' She lifted one shoulder in a shrug. 'You can't win them all.'

She felt him tense, felt the caressing hand halt its sensuous exploration, and closed her eyes instinctively against the sudden blaze in his. She was afraid he would strike her. The anger in him was almost tangible. But after a second's pause she felt him lift himself away from her.

She lay rigidly, her heart beating stormily, waiting for him to speak, steeling herself against the harsh words she knew she had provoked. But there wasn't a sound, and when she wonderingly opened her eyes, he was standing beside the bed looking down at her.

He said quite quietly, 'I'm going to take another shower, Lisa, to wash the scent of you, the taste of you off me. Don't be here when I get back.'

Nor had she been, Lisa thought wryly. And from that moment her every thought, her every action had been towards one purpose—to leave Stoniscliffe, to escape Dane Riderwood for ever.

And for a while she had almost succeeded, or that was how it seemed. But there was never really any escape. She had just been pretending to herself, in the same way she had tried to distance herself from reality by blocking it off in her mind.

Yet that had been a necessity. For months after she had left Stoniscliffe, after she had deliberately set out to make a new life for herself, she had been haunted by memories of Dane. The nights were worst. So many times she had woken, trembling, her whole body a mute agony of craving for the satisfaction which had been denied her. By day, she could control her thoughts, but at night her dreams were a different matter.

How many times, Lisa wondered, had she sat in bed, just as she was doing now, repeating over and over her litany of hate and shame trying to exorcise him from her mind? So many times, and yet she had never succeeded.

For here she was, one night back in the house, wide awake, every nerve, every sense attuned to the man pursuing his own lonely path outside in the darkness.

Lonely? She laughed in self-contempt. That was surely a romanticised view of the situation. Dane liked to walk at night. He always had. These solitary walks helped him see problems clearly, and she could only guess the problem that was keeping him from sleep tonight.

She slid back under the bedclothes with a little sigh. But lonely? She had never had the least reason to think that Dane of all people could be that. Just because he had invited no lady to dine with them that evening it didn't mean that there was no one. Dane had always had someone, she reminded herself, always. Someone who doubtless regarded him as an expert and exciting lover, who would find that slight edge of cruelty in him, that controlled violence, an extra stimulant.

As I might have myself, she confessed honestly, if I'd had the experience he assumed.

But as it was she had been terrified and ashamed. She had felt degraded and she knew that was what he had intended, and that had been the worst thing of all. He had cold-bloodedly decided that she was anybody's and treated her accordingly. And he still thought so, because she had deliberately let him retain that impression.

And I'll go on doing so, she thought, if that's the way to keep him at a distance. He thinks I'm living with someone as it is, and Julie's idiotic remarks about James Dalton went home too.

She turned over on to her face, shutting her eyes so tightly that they hurt.

She thought wretchedly, 'Oh God, let him hate me. Let him despise me if he must—if that's the only way I'm going to be safe.'

She must have slept after that, because the next thing she

knew it was daylight, and Julie was standing beside the bed, smiling and holding a cup of tea.

'This room's like an igloo,' she complained. 'I forgot you were a fresh air fiend.'

'Sorry.' Lisa sat up, accepting the cup. 'Wrap my dressing gown round you if you're staying.'

'Of course I'm staying,' Julie said airily. She perched on the side of the bed, and began to drink her own tea. 'Oh, Lisa, it's so lovely having you home! I've been so miserable over the past couple of years.'

'Miserable—making Tony fall in love with you?' Lisa teased gently.

'Oh,' Julie hunched a shoulder, 'I didn't mean that. But there was never anyone to talk to.'

'I thought you'd appointed Celia Dalton to the role of confidante.'

She saw Julie's eyes swivel towards her for a moment, and with real unguarded surprise in their depths, but then the moment passed and her stepsister was smiling again.

'She isn't as bad as you think.'

'I hope not,' Lisa said drily. 'And what the hell did you mean by giving everyone the impression that I was dying of love for James? You know perfectly well it's nonsense.'

Julie shrugged. 'I thought it might make Celia a little less smug for once. She's terribly possessive, you know.'

'And now she's out for my blood.' Lisa shook her head wryly. 'Thanks, friend.' She set her cup down on the bedside table. 'What's the programme for today?'

'Oh, we shan't be doing very much,' Julie said. She smiled mischievously. 'We've got to get you acclimatised slowly after your months in the effete South.'

'But that isn't why I came,' Lisa pointed out. 'I'm supposed to be helping you with this wedding, and we ought to make a start on the preparations—that is unless you're prepared to postpone the ceremony.'

'No, I'm not,' Julie said petulantly. 'Don't fuss, Lisa. Everything will get done in time. If you want, we can go over and look at the flat. Mama Bainbridge is always clucking at me to keep an eye on its progress. She seems to think I should supervise the placing of every light socket and plug.'

'Well, a lot of girls would want to,' Lisa said fairly. 'Not everyone has the chance of a tailor-made home to their own requirements.'

'Perhaps, but I think plumbing and wiring are incredibly dreary.' Julie finished her own tea and got up restlessly. 'Do you want the bathroom first?'

'Go ahead,' Lisa said promptly. She was vaguely troubled again, but couldn't have said why.

She thought, 'I'm being a fool. They love each other—I had the proof of that last night. There must be some small snag. I wish Julie would talk about it. I expect she's making mountains out of molehills.'

When she got down to the breakfast room, she was surprised that Julie wasn't there before her. Chas was already installed, however, with the maligned nurse, a sensible-looking woman with greying hair and glasses.

And Dane was there too, eating grilled bacon and mushrooms and tomatoes. Lisa half checked in the doorway when she saw him. Her re-creation of the events of two years ago had made them seem like yesterday all over again, and the sight of him seated quite calmly at the breakfast table was somehow shocking.

'So there you are, darling,' Chas hailed her jovially. 'I don't think you've met my stepdaughter,' he added, turning to the nurse. 'Lisa, this is Miss Henderson who looks after me, and makes me do my infernal exercises.'

'And I'm sure that isn't what you say behind my back,' Miss Henderson remarked serenely, shaking hands with Lisa.

Mrs Arkwright came in with a large pot of coffee which she set on the table.

'Will you have a cooked breakfast, Miss Lisa?' she asked.

'No, thanks,' Lisa shook her head. 'Just toast and coffee.'

Mrs Arkwright frowned disapprovingly, but made no comment. When she'd gone, Chas said, 'You ought to eat more, Lisa. I noticed at dinner last night, you just picked at your food. You're too thin as it is.'

Lisa smiled, 'I don't think Jos would agree with you.'

'And who is Jos?' It was Dane speaking, his mouth curling slightly.

'My photographer,' she returned coolly. 'Or at least the one I work with most.'

'And lovely pictures he takes,' Miss Henderson commented. 'You were the Amber Girl, weren't you, Miss Riderwood?'

Lisa was just nodding in confirmation, when Dane said, 'The name is Grayson—Lisa Grayson.'

'Oh,' Miss Henderson looked slightly embarrassed. 'Of course, I should have realised . . .'

'A technicality,' Chas said breezily. 'Lisa's a Riderwood in all but name, isn't that so, darling?'

Lisa forced a smile, aware of Dane's ironic glance. 'If you say so, Chas. Does anyone know where Julie is?'

'She's probably out walking. She often does before breakfast,' Chas said.

'Julie does?' Lisa's brows rose incredulously. She laughed a little shakily. 'My goodness, she has changed!'

'What did you expect?' Dane's eyes were fixed on her levelly. 'That everything here would be in a vacuum just waiting your return?'

'No, of course not.' She spoke sharply, nettled by his tone. 'Early morning walks aren't particularly characteristic of Julie, that's all.'

'Perhaps you regard them as your prerogative.' Dane

pushed his plate away and reached for the toast rack. 'Or have you changed as well, at least in that respect?'

How dared he? Lisa thought wildly. How dared he taunt her like this when he knew she was unable to defend herself because of the presence of Chas and the nurse?

She said with deliberate lightness, 'I haven't exactly been inhabiting a vacuum either.'

His eyes flicked over her like a whiplash. 'No,' was all he said.

At that moment Julie herself came in, eyes bright and cheeks glowing.

'Hello, everyone.' She almost danced round the table to kiss Chas and bestow a swift hug upon Lisa. 'Isn't it a beautiful day?'

'Wintry showers forecast for later on,' Miss Henderson said.

'Oh, I don't care what it does later on,' Julie laughed. 'As long as the sun shines on me in the morning.'

'And what are your plans for the sun while it shines?' Chas demanded indulgently.

'I'm going to take Lisa to look at the flat.' Julie helped herself to cereal.

Dane swallowed the last of his toast and rose. He said to his father, 'If Christopherson phones, will you tell him I'll be in Leeds all day?'

As Chas nodded, Julie leaned forward. 'Oh, Dane darling, if you're going to be in Leeds, we'll come down later and you can take us to lunch. It's been ages since you did that.'

He hesitated. His eyes were fixed on Julie. He did not even spare Lisa a glance. He said, 'Not today, Julie. I have a mountain of work facing me. Some other time, perhaps.'

Julie pouted, and Chas said, 'You can't turn down an offer like that, lad. You have to eat, after all, and a lunch date with two lovely girls will help the mountain of work along.'

Dane's face became grimmer than ever. He said coldly, 'Very well. Come to the office at twelve-thirty, Julie, and I'll see what I can arrange.'

She glowed at him. 'Darling, you're a wonderful brother —isn't he, Lisa?'

Lisa put down the piece of toast she had been trying to summon up some enthusiasm for, and murmured something indistinguishable, aware of Dane's ironic gaze. When she looked up, however, he had gone, and she was able to relax a little.

When the meal was over she put on a coat and accompanied Julie round to the garages at the side of the house where Julie's smart black Mini Metro was kept.

'Very nice,' Lisa remarked, running a hand over the gleaming paintwork.

Julie giggled. 'It was a reward,' she said airily. 'Daddy simply didn't believe I'd ever pass the test. But I did—at the fourth attempt.'

Watching Julie reverse out of the garage and turn in the drive, Lisa could only wonder that the fourth test had been successful. She crossed her fingers surreptitiously as she got into the passenger seat and they shot off down the drive.

The Bainbridges' house was set well back from the road, down a private access track punctuated by gates and cattle grids. It was a large gracious building constructed from the traditional local stone, with a large formal garden at the front. Most of the farm buildings, including the barn which was being converted for Tony and Julie, were at the rear of the property, but Julie did not drive straight round. She stopped in front of the house in a swirl of gravel, and a little screech of brakes, and looked at Lisa with a faint grimace.

'Come on,' she said. 'We'd better report for duty.'

The Bainbridges' housekeeper admitted them and led

them along a flagged passage to a large airy sitting room, furnished with flowered chintz. Mrs Bainbridge was sitting at a desk in the window writing, but she got up with a welcoming smile as the girls came in.

'Julie dear, how nice! We don't see nearly enough of you. And this is Lisa, of course. What a great success you've had. We've all followed your career with great interest locally.'

'I now declare this bazaar open,' Julie murmured in an undertone to Lisa as Mrs Bainbridge turned to the house-keeper to ask for coffee to be brought.

Lisa gave her a quelling frown and resigned herself to at least half an hour's chat about her life as a model. She had never disliked Mrs Bainbridge, although she could under-stand the haphazard Julie being irritated by her serene efficiency. It was epitomised by the spotless room, the log fire burning brightly in the burnished grate, the bowls of bulbs on the windowsills and side tables.

Over coffee, Mrs Bainbridge said, 'I was hoping to tele-phone you, Julie. They're almost at the stage of tiling the kitchen and bathroom, and I've had some samples delivered of those I thought most suitable. You don't have to choose any of them, naturally, dear. There are plenty of catalogues available. Did you have a look through any of those I gave you?'

Julie gave a negligent shrug. 'I haven't had time, I'm afraid. I'm sure whatever you've picked will be fine.'

'But I haven't picked anything, dear,' Mrs Bainbridge said rather repressively. 'It's for you and Tony to choose. It's your home, after all. I've left the samples at the flat, and all you have to do is decide and let the foreman know your choice.' She gave a little sigh. 'I had hoped Tony would be here this morning, but he's had to go into Skipton with his father.'

'Well, it doesn't matter.' Julie put her empty coffee cup back on the table. 'I only wanted to show Lisa the flat.

Come on, Lisa, we'd better make a start. We have to be in Leeds for twelve-thirty, don't forget.'

As they made their way across the courtyard at the back of the house, Lisa said, 'Julie, you were really rude just now.'

'Well, it's all so silly,' Julie said defensively. 'She knows quite well that she'll be picking the tiles in the end, just as she's chosen everything else. Oh, it's all done very charmingly, but everything I like is always "Rather unsuitable, dear", and as they're paying for it, that's the end of the discussion.' She paused. 'Well, here we are.'

On the face of it, the conversion seemed to be a good one. The ground floor had been used for garaging, a reception area and a cloakroom, and then a pine staircase ascended to a large studio sitting room with stunning views of the dale. The kitchen was big enough to eat in, and as well as the small bathroom there were two reasonably sized bedrooms.

There was little doubt that the flat would be ready for Tony and Julie to move into as soon as they were married, Lisa thought, looking round. Most of the current work was in the kitchen where a range of luxury units, including a built-in oven and ceramic hob, were being installed. Lisa had expected Julie to linger, but she only gave them a cursory glance before wandering back into the sitting room.

'I suppose these are the tiles she means,' she said, glancing at a large cardboard box on the floor. 'What do you think of them, Lisa?'

'I think you should look at them and make up your own mind,' Lisa said roundly. 'You're going to have to live with them, after all.'

'Yes, I am,' Julie muttered almost savagely. 'With all of them.' She went across to the big picture window and stared out. Lisa noticed that the first golden promise of the morning had faded, and that dark slate-coloured clouds were gathering.

She joined Julie at the window. 'It looks like snow,' she commented neutrally. 'What a terrific view.'

'Isn't it just?' Julie agreed with a little laugh. 'And the views from the other windows are even better. Look!' She crossed the room and stuck out a hand with a dramatic gesture.

'It's the main house,' Lisa said after a pause. The note in Julie's voice worried her.

'Yes, the main house,' Julie said. 'Here we are, quite separate, quite self-contained, as Mama Bainbridge is so fond of pointing out, and yet we're never out of sight. *Thou, God, seest me.*' She gave an uneven giggle. 'What a prospect!'

'Oh, come on,' Lisa urged. 'You're a good distance from the house—much farther in fact than you'd be from your neighbours on a new estate.'

'She watches,' Julie said. 'Every time I've been here, she's watched. She's even waved to me once or twice. Can you imagine what it will be like when I'm actually living here?'

'Oh, Julie!' Lisa sighed ruefully. 'She's probably— anxious. She wants to help, to make sure that everything's perfect for you. Tony's her only son, after all.'

'Don't I know it,' Julie said mutinously.

'Julie.' Lisa put her hands on her stepsister's shoulders and looked worried at her. 'If this is how you feel, don't you think you should postpone the wedding for a while— give yourself time to be sure?'

Julie shook off her grasp almost pettishly. 'What are you talking about? I am sure, and I'm marrying Tony as arranged. It's just that his mother gets me down rather.'

'Then is it impossible for you to find somewhere else to live?' Lisa urged gently. 'If you really feel you'll be living in Mrs Bainbridge's pocket . . .'

'It's all right, I tell you. I'll get used to it.' Julie walked across to the box of tiles and pulled some of them out. 'I should think these would do for the kitchen, wouldn't you? And these gold patterned ones for the bathroom. I'll give them to the foreman, and then we can get off to Leeds.'

Lisa sighed. 'Do you really think that's such a good idea? Dane clearly didn't want us to go.'

Julie waved an airy hand. 'Oh, it does Dane good to be thwarted occasionally. Besides, I want to go to Leeds. It would be a good opportunity to look for a wedding dress.'

'I thought you were going to some boutique in Skipton,' Lisa said rather wearily.

'Well, perhaps I shall. But we can look in Leeds first.' Julie put a placatory hand on Lisa's arm. 'Oh, darling, am I a terrible problem to you?'

'As always.' Lisa smiled at her wryly.

'We'll go back to the house and change,' Julie planned happily. 'You can wear something that will knock Dane's eye out. It's time you two buried the hatchet, whatever you quarrelled about. I'm sure he fancies you secretly. He didn't like it when I was teasing you about James.'

'I don't care for it myself,' said Lisa. 'But please don't let that vivid imagination loose on Dane and me.' She added in a constrained voice, 'We're really quite happy with our mutual antipathy.'

'But you shouldn't be,' Julie said petulantly. 'You're gorgeous, Lisa. All those magazine pictures were dazzling. And Dane's incredibly sexy—even I can see that.'

Lisa moistened her lips. 'Julie, whatever equation you're working out in your head, forget it.' She gave a little nervous laugh. 'You can't just add people together and come up with the desired result, you know. And the fact is that Dane and I have never—liked each other.'

'But I want you to like each other,' Julie said stubbornly. 'And Chas does too. When he heard that you were coming home and Dane was bringing you, he was delighted, and he said that the dearest wish of his heart was . . .'

'Julie, please!' Lisa interrupted sharply. 'I don't want to hear about it. I don't even want to discuss it any further. The whole thing is ridiculous, and if you persist, I shan't come to Leeds. In fact, I'll go back to London on the next train.'

'All right, I won't say another word,' Julie promised penitently, but she gave Lisa a puzzled glance.

To Lisa's relief, Julie kept her promise and chatted about all kinds of things on the way back to the house, and later on the journey to Leeds. But it wasn't a peaceful trip by any means. Julie's driving was erratic to say the least, and Lisa was constantly on edge. She breathed a silent sigh of thankfulness when Julie turned the car through the high wrought iron gates which led to the Riderwood works, and parked it with more panache than expertise in front of the main office block.

She walked confidently into the reception area, calling a greeting to the girls who worked there.

'Tell Mr Riderwood we're on our way up,' she threw over her shoulder as she headed for the lift.

The offices upstairs hadn't changed a great deal since the days when Chas had been there, Lisa thought, remembering nostalgically how Jennifer had used to bring her there to see him when she was a child. She could recall how he had sat her down in a swivel chair which rose miraculously, the faster he turned it, and how Miss Palmer, his elderly secretary, had given her peppermints from a tin in her desk drawer, and let her type her name very slowly and importantly at the big, glossy electric typewriter.

There were still the tall filing cabinets, the expanse of plain moss green carpet, and the dark oak solid desks with the gleaming brass handles.

But no Miss Palmer, of course, and Lisa doubted whether the slim chic blonde who sat behind the very latest model in electric typewriters would have anything as plebeian as peppermints in her desk drawers. Turkish Delight, perhaps, she thought, and a spare bottle of Chanel Number Five.

Dane was on the phone, so they had to wait for a few minutes. Julie began to chat to the secretary in her ebullient way, while Lisa wandered over to the window and stood looking out. There was a hint of snow in the air. A few flakes drifted past the glass as she watched, and she hoped that it would not amount to much. Julie's performance on reasonably dry roads was bad enough. What she would be like in icy conditions didn't bear thinking about.

The door at the other side of the room opened, and Dane said brusquely, 'I've booked a table at the Wharfe Court for one, so we'd better hurry. Are you ready?'

Lisa turned hastily, flurried by his sudden appearance and by the impatience in his voice, and her hand caught a pile of folders on the edge of the desk, sending them flying to the ground.

'Oh!' she exclaimed distressfully and knelt to retrieve them. There were sheets and sheets, all covered in figures, and Dane said, 'Leave them. Miss Cartwright will see to them.'

She got slowly to her feet, aware that she had flushed a dull red.

She said, 'I wasn't prying.'

'Of course not. Just taking a healthy interest in the family business. Well, you can reassure yourself and all other interested parties that Riderwoods are not suffering particularly from the present recession,' he said caustically. 'In case that was what was worrying you.'

'It wasn't,' she said. 'It really isn't any of my business.'

'Except that it pays the allowance my father gives you,' he said. 'And there's no need to look embarrassed—Miss Cartwright knows all about that. She's the person who arranges for the transfer of the money each month.'

'Then I can save her at least one irksome task,' Lisa said. She was trembling with anger. 'Please cancel the allowance, as of now. I don't need your money.'

'I don't suppose you do.' His eyes slid cynically over her, taking in the elegance of the dark green velvet suit with its bloused jacket and the matching high-necked sweater. 'But no doubt you'll find a use for it just the same. Besides, it's my father's wish that it should be paid, not mine, so if you want to make any alteration in the arrangements you'll have to talk to him.'

Lisa was almost numb with outrage as she followed him out of the office and to the lift. Even Julie shot her a sympathetic glance.

When they reached the car, Julie objected to sitting in the front as Lisa wanted.

'Lisa should sit there,' she protested. 'After all, she's really the guest today. I'm only your sister.'

'I wasn't aware that either of you were my guests,' Dane said rather grimly. 'Perhaps if one or the other of you would like to get in the car, we can go and have lunch.'

Julie scrambled into the back, giving Lisa a victorious look, while her stepsister got reluctantly into the passenger seat. She stared rigidly ahead of her as they drove out to the village where the Wharfe Court was situated.

It was a charming spot, Lisa had to admit, as they drove in. A small country house with an adjoining coach-house which had been skilfully converted into a hotel and restaurant. And in more congenial company, she thought furiously, she could probably have looked forward to her meal very much. As it was, she barely gave the menu a glance, ordering clear soup and a grilled sole to the head waiter's obvious disappointment. Dane said briefly, 'I'll have the same,' but Julie was not to be hurried, eventually choosing melon and steak cooked in red wine and mushrooms.

The bar was already over half full as they sat sipping their aperitifs and waiting to be called to their table, and a lot of the people present were known to Dane and Julie, who were constantly acknowledging greetings. Lisa herself was the recipient of a number of sideways glances, but she ignored them. She was becoming used to this form of semi-recognition and it no longer bothered her a great deal. She was amused by the number of men who stopped by their table on one pretext or another, and whom Dane had, perforce, to introduce to her.

'Going around with Lisa is a bit like a royal progress,' Julie remarked as they went to their table in the dining room. 'Heads turn as she goes by.'

'So I notice,' Dane said coldly.

'You are grumpy today, darling,' Julie said reproach-fully. 'Are you still cross with us for inviting ourselves to lunch? But you didn't have anyone else to take out. Tina's still in Bermuda, isn't she?'

He said briefly, 'Yes,' and turned to confer with the wine waiter.

'So the current lady's name is Tina,' Lisa thought, straightening a knife with mathematical precision.

She found herself imagining what this unknown Tina was like. Blonde, she supposed. Dane had always had a predilection for blondes. And from the same sort of wealthy background as himself. That was the usual pattern.

'Did you go to see the flat?' Dane was addressing her, his tone cool and formal, as if she were some stranger to whom he was forced to show politeness.

'Why, yes. I think it will be charming,' Lisa returned with equal studied courtesy.

He shrugged. 'If it's what Julie wants.'

But is it? Lisa wanted to say. Why don't we all lay our cards on the table and find out just what it is that Julie wants? You're her brother, after all. Why doesn't she confide in you, even if she doesn't want to worry Chas?

But they were bringing the first course, and she had perforce to remain silent.

It was a difficult meal. Dane was taciturn, joining in Julie's bright babble of conversation with an obvious effort. For Lisa the whole thing was taking on a curious air of unreality. All of us are playing parts, she thought. Not one of us is saying what we're really thinking.

She had hardly tasted a mouthful of the delicious food placed in front of her, and when the sweet trolley made its appearance, she chose a small portion of fresh fruit salad, without cream.

'Watching your figure again, love?' Julie laughed. 'You really needn't, you know.'

'That's what you think,' Lisa retorted. 'The people who hire me have an eagle eye for an extra pound'!

'Including this Jos?' said Dane, selecting some cheese from the board in front of him.

'Among others.' His tone nettled her, and she spoke more shortly than she had intended.

His eyes were as cold and forbidding as the skies outside the window. 'He's married, I take it.'

'He is.' Lisa spooned up some of the pineapple and grapes in her salad with every appearance of enjoyment. She smiled. 'But of course I don't allow that to make any difference.'

That was perfectly true, she thought judiciously. All she'd done was alter the emphasis a little. In fact, ironically, Jos had always been like an older brother to her, filling the place that Dane had scorned. And yet was brotherhood the role she really wanted him to play in her life? she thought painfully.

She was behaving stupidly and she knew it, but what did it matter? Dane despised her. He always had and always would, so nothing she said or did would make very much difference.

Julie leaned forward. 'What's this? Has poor James got a rival?' She clapped her hand over her mouth, her dancing eyes both mischievous and penitent. 'Oh, Lisa, I'm sorry. I know you told me not to talk about him . . .'

'That isn't quite what I meant,' Lisa said, wondering rather bitterly how she could have forgotten Julie's propensity for mischief.

Dane said acidly, 'I gather he has a number of rivals,' and signalled to the waiter to bring their coffee.

'Well, they say there's safety in numbers,' said Lisa with a lightness she did not feel.

Numbers, she thought wearily, remembering the aridity of her life over the past two years. It was almost amusing. She thought of Simon and their cautious, almost negative relationship, and sighed.

Julie was saying, 'Lisa's dragging me round the shops this afternoon to look at wedding dresses.'

'Then I'd better drop you near the shopping centre,' said Dane, finishing the last of his coffee, and signing the bill. 'Are you ready?' He didn't look at Lisa.

'Quite ready,' Julie affirmed, pushing her cup away almost untouched with a little grimace. 'Doesn't this coffee taste bitter?'

Lisa stood alone in the foyer. Julie had gone to the powder room and Dane was fetching his coat from the cloakroom. She didn't hear him approach on the thickly carpeted floor, and she gasped out loud when his hand descended on her shoulder.

He said grimly, 'I'm warning you, Lisa. Play your sordid little games in London if you must, but not here. I won't have any local scandals upsetting my father and clouding my sister's wedding. Is that clearly understood?'

'I understand only too well.' She made no attempt to hide

her bitterness, her eyes wary and hostile. His hand fell away from her and she walked towards the swing doors, leading to the car park.

The wind had freshened and flurries of snow were whirling down from the leaden sky. Lisa paused instinctively, as the wind caught her breath, making her draw her coat more closely about her, and slightly off balance, she swayed backwards, colliding with Dane who had followed her out. At the same moment the wind lifted her loose cloud of hair, blowing it back across Dane's face.

For a few seconds he did not move, but stood rigidly, then with a muttered expletive he tore at the soft strands blowing across his mouth and cheek. He was very white, and a muscle was jerking furiously near his jaw.

He said harshly, 'God damn you, Lisa, why did you have to come back into our lives?'

Then he strode away towards the car, leaving her standing there alone in the cold dank wind.

CHAPTER SEVEN

LISA had almost recovered her composure by the time she and Julie reached the bridal department of the large department store which was their first port of call.

Dane had said little as he had driven into the city, beyond tersely telling Julie to get a taxi back to Stoniscliffe if the weather became too bad, and he would arrange for her car to be brought back for her. He hadn't said a word to Lisa, or even looked at her, but she had been as conscious of him as if he had taken her in his arms, touched her, kissed her.

Those few seconds when her body had rested against his had been a shattering experience, even though it had been the most fleeting, the most grudging of contacts.

But she mustn't think about that, she told herself, as she looked around her at the satin, the lace, the chiffon—at the wax models with their unrealistic poses and their bright, exaggerated smiles.

I could take the place of any one of them, she thought.

A pleasant middle-aged saleswoman had appeared, and was asking if she could be of assistance.

Julie said, 'I'd like to see a selection of wedding dresses, please. I'm size ten.'

They were shown into a mirrored changing room, and the saleswoman hung up Julie's coat and dress and helped her change her boots for a pair of high-heeled white satin shoes. Then she produced a tape measure.

Julie said rather irritably, 'There's no need for that, surely. I've told you I wear size ten. I always have.'

The saleswoman murmured something deferential about

wanting to make sure, and passed the tape measure swiftly and expertly round Julie's bust, waist and hips, then vanished.

'How ridiculous,' said Julie. 'We might look and see if they have any bridesmaids' dresses while we're here. Perhaps something in green.'

'It's supposed to be unlucky,' said Lisa.

'I don't believe in superstition,' Julie said scornfully. 'You can make your own luck.'

At that moment the saleslady returned, together with another assistant, bearing reverently swathed drifts of white in their arms.

'Hm,' Julie eyed them thoughtfully as they were displayed in turn. 'What do you think, Lisa?'

'The chiffon is charming,' Lisa said consideringly. 'I like the lace too. But I'd keep away from satin, if I were you.'

'I'll try the chiffon,' Julie announced. 'Let me have a closer look at it.' She began to examine the detail on the dress, the soft swathing of the bodice, the tiny pearl buttons that fastened the deep tight-fitting cuffs beneath the billowing sleeves. Then Lisa saw her stiffen, and that dangerous sparkle come into her eyes.

She said, 'I think there's been some mistake. This is a size twelve, and I told you quite distinctly that I was a ten.'

The saleswoman looked apologetic. 'I'm sorry, madam, but I did measure you. I think we all put on a little weight without noticing it in the winter. If you'd just try the dress.'

Julie said between gritted teeth, 'I have not put on any weight. I won't try on a dress which isn't my size. It's just a waste of time. If you won't bring my correct size, just say so, and I'll go elsewhere.'

'It's quite all right, madam.' The saleswoman was flushed,

but dignified. 'I'll bring the ten.' She withdrew rather huffily.

Lisa said sharply, 'Julie, for heaven's sake behave yourself! Perhaps your measurements have altered slightly . . .'

'Of course they haven't,' Julie denied hotly. 'There must be something wrong with her stupid tape measure.'

'Well, I still think it's a pity you didn't let Mrs Langthwaite make your dress. She's a superb fitter and . . .'

'No!' Julie came perilously near to stamping her foot. 'I won't have her anywhere near me—nosy gossipy woman!'

'Weddings do tend to be rather public affairs,' Lisa reminded her gently.

'Well, mine won't be,' Julie said grimly. She paused, putting a hand to her head. 'It's awfully hot in here. I wish that woman would hurry.'

'You shouldn't be too warm,' Lisa said with a derisive glance at Julie's scanty half-cup bra, and the lace-trimmed waist slip.

'It's just terribly stuffy,' Julie's voice was defensive. 'Don't you feel it?'

'Not particularly.' Lisa turned. 'Oh, here's your dress.'

The saleswoman was smiling again, probably inured to Julie's display of temper by years of bridal tantrums, Lisa thought.

'This is the size ten, madam. Shall we just slip it on? There we are. Now, there's a concealed zip and a row of masking buttons at the back. Let me just . . .' She tugged at the zip, moving it upwards a few inches. Lisa saw her exchange a speaking glance with her assistant, then apply herself once more to the zip. It was obvious to anyone that the dress was too tight. In fact Lisa doubted whether it would ever fasten without ripping.

She said hastily, 'I think that's enough for my sister to see what the effect would be.'

'It's perfectly delightful,' the saleslady agreed, stepping

back. 'And in the right size . . .'

'This is the right size!' Julie almost raged. 'You haven't even tried to do it up yet. You're just making a fuss because you don't like to be wrong.'

The saleslady's expression said plainly that she didn't consider that it was herself making the fuss, but her voice was smooth and polite. The dress was an expensive model, the fabric was extremely fragile, any undue pressure might prove disastrous.

'Then take it off,' Julie ordered imperiously. 'Take it away—take all of them away. I don't like any of them.'

Lisa was on the point of apologising when a muffled cry from the younger assistant stopped her, and she turned in time to see a very white-faced Julie sway with a hand to her head, then slide noiselessly to the fluffy beige carpet.

They were very kind and competent. Someone brought a glass of water and between them they managed to get Julie on to one of the satin-covered chairs from the showroom. Someone else at Lisa's request went to order a taxi to take them home.

She herself knelt at Julie's side, holding her hand. At last Julie's eyelids fluttered and a little colour returned to her face.

She said, 'Lisa, I don't want to buy any dresses today. I— I feel so sick.'

'We'll go home,' Lisa said steadily. 'Don't try to talk.' Her mouth felt dry suddenly. She had seen the meaning look the saleslady had just given her assistant and interpreted it without the slightest difficulty.

Julie, she thought wildly. My God, could it be true?

There was no opportunity to talk privately in the taxi, even if Julie had been in any fit state to do so. She was still very pale, and spent most of the journey huddled into her corner of the rear seat, with her eyes closed.

But when they reached Stoniscliffe there would have to be

some sort of confrontation, Lisa thought unhappily.

As the taxi drew up in front of the main door, Mrs Arkwright appeared, looking slightly alarmed.

'Miss Julie! Is anything wrong?'

'Just a slight dizzy spell.' Lisa made her voice sound reassuring. 'Perhaps you'd fill a hot water bottle for her, Mrs Arkwright, while I take her up to her room. Where's Mr Riderwood? I don't want him to be worried.'

'He's having his rest,' Mrs Arkwright returned, her gaze still fixed anxiously on Julie. 'She does look pale. Shall I make some tea for her?'

'Yes, that would be splendid,' said Lisa, wondering whether Julie would complain about its bitterness as she had about the coffee at lunch.

She got Julie up to her room, removed her boots and coaxed her to lie down under the quilt. Mrs Arkwright arrived with the bottle and the tray of tea, and it took all of Lisa's diplomacy to get her out of the room again.

She went and sat on the edge of the bed where Julie was lying with her eyes closed. She said gently but firmly, 'It's time for the truth, Julie. You're pregnant, aren't you?'

Julie's eyes flew open. She said hoarsely, 'I don't know what you're talking about.'

'I think you do.' Lisa was relentless. 'It explains everything—your gain in weight, your moods, your lack of appetite, your fainting fit. And of course the great rush to get married. And I suppose why you didn't want Mrs Langthwaite to make your wedding dress. You were afraid she might suspect something.'

'Of course she would. She never misses anything.' Julie's hand clutched at Lisa's. 'And she mustn't know— no one must know. They don't have to. The wedding's so close, and babies—first babies—are premature sometimes aren't they, Lisa?'

She could hear the frightened voice of a much younger

Julie saying, 'There's nothing in the dark, is there, Lisa? There aren't any bogey men who'll come for me if I don't go to sleep?'

'Aren't they?' Julie pleaded again.

Lisa sighed. 'I don't know, darling. Perhaps. And will it really matter, anyway? These things happen, and you and Tony are going to be married. I don't think a great many eyebrows will be raised.'

'But it does matter,' Julie said rapidly, clinging to Lisa's hand. 'I don't want anyone to know.'

Lisa gave her a rueful smile. 'But people do know. I know for one, and of course there's Tony . . .'

'No,' said Julie.

'I don't understand,' Lisa stared at her.

Julie moistened her lips with the tip of her tongue. 'I— I haven't told him.'

'But why not?' Lisa demanded in amazement. 'Darling, he has a right to know. You must see that. Do you think it would make any difference? You know he adores you.'

'Yes,' Julie said, 'I know. But I just don't want him to know—about the baby.' She shivered suddenly. 'I didn't want anyone to know but me.'

Lisa gave her a troubled look. She supposed she understood. Tony might tell his mother, and Mrs Bainbridge would disapprove. She would not be able to help it, and it would show in her attitude to Julie, and heaven knew things were strained enough between them as it was. She could believe Julie would want her future mother-in-law kept in the dark until she and Tony were married, and the news of a baby could be greeted with universal rejoicing.

She bent and kissed Julie lightly on the cheek. 'Try and get some sleep, love, and above all don't get yourself into another state. It's not good for you, or the baby.'

'Lisa,' Julie's fingers tightened round hers momentarily, then relaxed, 'I'm so glad you're here. I'm so glad you came home—I really needed you.'

Lisa smiled at her. 'That's good. It's nice to be needed.'

On her way downstairs to phone the works and tell Dane
—or more probably his secretary—that Julie would not be
collecting her car, she realised that she meant what she
had said. It was nice to be needed by someone. She had never
fooled herself. She had been lonely quite often, especially
after her mother had remarried, and she was no longer first
in her life. They had been mutually dependent until Chas
came on the scene, and although she had never grudged her
mother's happiness, not for a minute, she had sometimes
thought wistfully of the old days. And the Farrells had
never needed her, except as the occasional provider of
goodies. Simon? She wondered but could come to no firm
decision. If she hadn't been relatively well-known—a face,
in other words, would he have bothered with her? Certainly
their relationship didn't have a lot going for it as far as he
was concerned. The Amber Girl could have been re-
christened the Ice Maiden, she thought with a grimace.

But she wasn't sure it was right for her to be needed by
Julie. It should be Tony she was turning to right now. It
should be Tony's hand she was clinging to. She wondered if
she ought to talk to him, but Julie had been so definite about
not wanting him to know. It was hard to know what to do
for the best.

She dialled the works number and asked for Dane's
office. She was expecting Miss Cartwright to answer and it
was a shock when Dane's voice said, 'Yes?'

She said breathlessly, 'It's Lisa. We—we came home early
from shopping because Julie wasn't too well. I thought
should let you know.'

He said laconically, 'So you've let me know. What's the
matter with Julie?'

'I don't know,' she lied. 'Maybe 'flu. It's the time of
year for it.' And she thought, what am I doing here chattering

inanities, when there are so many other things I ought to say, if only I could find the words.

He said, 'Perhaps. Tell her not to worry about the car. And would you be good enough to tell Mrs Arkwright that I won't be at home for dinner.'

'I'll tell her,' she said with a kind of insane brightness in her voice. 'Goodbye, Dane,' and she rang off too quickly to know whether he had responded to her valediction.

As she turned away from the telephone to relay his message, she wondered why he wasn't coming home for dinner. A business appointment, perhaps, or something more personal? Not Tina, she reminded herself, with a faint grimace. Tina was in Bermuda, but that didn't mean that Dane necessarily had a gap in his life. There would be someone else, maybe even several someones.

And she found herself wondering what it would be like to be one of them. To be Lisa Grayson, complete stranger, meeting Dane Riderwood, ditto, at a party or a point-to-point, and accepting his invitation to dinner. To be with him without shadows. To know a beginning instead of the bitterness of an ending. To be in his arms. To know the pleasure instead of the pain of loving.

She whispered, 'And to know that he needed me, even if it was only for a little while, even if it didn't last.'

It wasn't much to ask for, at that, but Lisa knew she might as well have been crying for the moon, and the knowledge was like a hand closing round her heart.

The next few days passed uneventfully enough. Julie passed off her indisposition lightly as being due to the wine she had drunk at lunch, and no one pressed the point.

One afternoon the two girls drove to Skipton, and Julie bought her wedding dress in the boutique she had mentioned previously. It was a pretty dress in a crisp fabric, with insertions of broderie anglaise on the bodice and sleeves, and Julie seemed pleased with it. And this time, Lisa noted thankfully, she asked for size twelve.

They were walking down the main street, looking at the market stalls, when a man's voice greeted them. Looking round, Lisa saw with some surprise that it was James Dalton.

'James!' Julie's face lit up. 'How lovely to see you. But what on earth are you doing here?'

'Visiting a customer,' he said. 'And you?'

'Just some shopping,' Julie said casually, and Lisa waited for her to mention her wedding dress, but instead she went on, 'We were just going to have some tea. Have you got time?'

'Always,' he said, smiling, and stationed himself between them. 'I think this must be my lucky day.'

'Why are you visiting customers?' Julie asked once they were ensconced behind a laden tea table. 'I thought you were much too important to do things like that.'

He pulled a slight face. 'Nominally, yes. In practice, I do what I'm told.'

Lisa studied him covertly as he chatted to Julie. He was extremely attractive, she decided, but there was a basic weakness about his mouth and chin which she hadn't noticed in her younger days. He probably didn't have an easy life, she thought fair-mindedly, recalling Celia's petulant beauty, and her sharp domineering manner towards him, but then she had never been any different, and he must have known that when he married her. If he had thought he was opting for the easy life, he knew better now.

Odd to think, she told herself wryly, that there had once been a time when she would have had butterflies at the mere prospect of sharing afternoon tea with James Dalton. In those days, she had had an idealised, romantic view of love, but no longer. Dane had smashed those ideals for ever.

She picked up her tea and swallowed some of it, trying to ease the sudden aching tightness in her throat. How wise she had been to close him out of her life and out of her mind for so long. It was bad enough to have to endure the sheer mental agony of reflecting how disastrously wrong their relationship had gone, but she hadn't bargained for the strong physical reaction she suffered each time his name was mentioned.

She was still deep in her own painful thoughts as they all walked back towards the car park, and she was startled to hear Julie's sudden impatient exclamation.

'Oh, damn! Lisa, I've left my stupid gloves on the table in the café. I'll have to go back for them,' she concluded wearily.

'No, you wait for me in the car. I'll go,' Lisa said swiftly, noticing that Julie was looking tired and rather pale.

She hurried back to the tea rooms, but a prolonged search revealed no sign of the gloves, and eventually she came across them in the boutique where they had bought Julie's wedding dress. Lisa pushed them hurriedly into her shoulder bag with a word of thanks and almost ran to the car park.

But there was no sign of the black Metro, she realised as soon as she arrived. Instead James detached himself almost apologetically from a large green Rover and came over to her.

'Julie had to go on, I'm afraid,' he said. 'She remembered she had an appointment to see the Vicar. Something to do with flowers for the ceremony, I gather, so she asked me if I'd bring you back.'

Lisa could have screamed with vexation, but she summoned up a polite smile and a word of thanks as she climbed into the passenger seat.

If it hadn't seemed totally ridiculous, she could almost have suspected Julie of manoeuvring her into James's company. After all, it was the first she had heard of any appointment with the Vicar. Most of the details about the wedding had already been decided on, as far as she knew. After Julie's teasing remarks about her former crush on James, it was almost embarrassing to be forced into his company like this.

At least James seemed equally embarrassed, if that was any consolation. They exchanged a few desultory remarks about the weather—the likelihood of the almost daily snow showers turning into a serious fall—and the differences between living and working in Yorkshire and London. James, she thought, sounded faintly envious.

'Doesn't your father-in-law's company have a London office?' Lisa asked eventually. 'Surely you could get a transfer there?'

He shrugged slightly, his face gloomy. 'Not as easy as it sounds. They are often regarded as plum jobs—rewards for good behaviour. I don't think I'd qualify.'

'Heavens!' Lisa said in mock dismay. 'What have you been doing?'

'Sins of omission,' he said lightly. 'At least, I think that's how you'd describe them. Failure to apply myself one hundred per cent to the job in hand. And, more seriously, failing to provide old Levison with a grandson and heir.'

'Oh,' Lisa said a little helplessly. 'But surely it's early days yet. You and Celia haven't been married all those many years. You'll probably end up having six children.'

'I very much doubt it,' James said cynically, and Lisa made haste to change the subject, uneasily aware that she had come close to trespassing on forbidden ground, although she hadn't lacked for encouragement from James. His marital difficulties, and it was clear that they existed, were no business of hers, however.

They had both relapsed into an uncomfortable silence by the time they reached Stoniscliffe, and Lisa could only be glad the trip was over. James drew up in front of the house, where Lisa went through the formality of thanking him for driving her home, and inviting him in for a drink which he declined as she had quite expected him to do.

Honour is satisfied, she thought, turning away with a slight smile, and registering in the same moment with a swift unpleasant shock that another car had followed James's vehicle into the drive—a car that she had begun to know only too well.

'Oh, damn and blast!' Lisa muttered savagely under her breath, and dived into the house, leaving Dane and James to exchange greetings. Brief greetings, however, because before she had reached the top of the stairs, Dane had appeared in the hall below.

'Lisa.' His voice was pitched low, but there was no mistaking the undercurrent of anger in it. 'Will you come down here, please? I'd like a word with you.' She hesitated, and he added smoothly, 'Please don't put me to the trouble of fetching you, Lisa.'

Stonily, she turned and walked down the stairs, passing in front of him to enter the study. He followed her in, tossing the brief case he held on to the desk. His face was dark and forbidding as he studied her.

He said, 'You don't listen, do you, Lisa, either to hints or to warnings. How many times have you to be told that James Dalton isn't for you?'

Her voice shook a little. 'And how often do I have to say that I haven't the slightest interest in him?'

'I doubt whether his wife would find your assurances particularly acceptable,' he said. 'She might wonder why you'd chosen to spend the afternoon in his company—and how James can spare the time from his work to roam around the countryside with you.'

'It's so easy to make assumptions, isn't it, Dane?' she asked tautly. 'I have not spent the afternoon with

James. I was with Julie up to half an hour ago in Skipton, but she left me stranded there, and I had to either accept James's offer of a lift or hang around possibly for hours waiting for a bus.'

'You just ran into James by chance?' His mouth curled slightly in disbelief. 'And Julie, of course, decided to play Cupid. I wonder whose idea that was?'

Lisa was a little taken aback. Could that really have been Julie's motive? Surely she didn't genuinely believe that Lisa was still carrying some kind of pathetic torch for James?

'It certainly wasn't mine.' She lifted her chin and looked back at him defiantly. 'James doesn't impress me on second acquaintance.'

'Of course not. The Amber Girl can afford to take her pick, and James is too much of a loser for a mercenary, self-seeking little bitch like you.'

She was almost stunned by the savagery of his words.

'Thanks,' she said faintly after a moment. 'May I go now, please, or have you some more insults to fling at me?'

'The truth hurts, does it?' he said inimically.

'The truth,' she repeated, shuddering. 'What would you know about that?'

'I know all I need to know about you, Lisa. I had the benefit of studying the subject at close quarters over a number of years, if you remember. And in spite of all the indications, you almost had me fooled for a while. I even began to think . . .' He hesitated, then his jaw clamped, and she saw that tiny muscle working almost convulsively. 'But that doesn't matter now.'

'How right you are,' she said, white with temper. 'Your opinion of me couldn't matter less. I always hated you, always knew you for an arrogant, uncaring swine. How I could ever have been fool enough to let you near me . . .'

'Let me!' he interrupted derisively. 'Don't make it sound as if you were a queen granting her favours, Lisa. Let's remember it as it was. You were as hot for me as I was for you. It was a revelation. Of course, if I'd been thinking clearly, I'd have realised exactly what it revealed—that any man could have extracted the same response—even a promiscuous, perverted little bastard like Laurie Hammond.'

His words fell like hammer blows on her wincing consciousness, but she refused to let him know he was hurting her.

'Why, Dane,' she made her voice poisonously sweet, 'you wouldn't be jealous of poor Laurie, would you?'

She saw his fist clench, and stiffened, wondering whether the violence in his voice was going to become physical reality.

'No, darling,' he said at last, very silkily. 'Not of him, or any other poor fools who've benefited from your—generosity. I just don't want James to become one of them. He's a friend, and I don't think he could cope when he finds out it's not real.'

'What isn't real?' She was a fool to ask, she thought wearily.

'The way you look, Lisa. Those innocent eyes, and that passionate mouth. Eve must have looked like that when Adam woke in Paradise and found her beside him. But you're no Eve, my lovely one, you're Lilith—the bitch goddess with the face like an angel and the soul of a whore.' His hand lifted and took her chin, gripping it so tightly that she wondered dazedly whether her face would be bruised tomorrow. 'I don't care how many men you have in London, Lisa, or what kind of a life you lead there. But here you'll behave. Neither Chas nor Julie are going to be made to suffer because there's more talk about you that could get back to them.'

'More talk?' She wrenched herself free. 'Would you like to explain exactly what you're talking about?'

'I'm talking about two years ago,' he said coldly. 'Did you really imagine your visits to the Hammonds and others would really go unnoticed? That someone in this relatively small community wouldn't notice, wouldn't have a quiet word, drop a hint that I ought to keep a closer eye on my womenfolk. And do you know, Lisa, I really didn't believe it. I think I actually laughed, and said there must be some mistake. I discounted the rumours, the sidelong looks and the veiled allusions. Even when I saw you with my own eyes walking back from their house in broad daylight, I tried to tell myself that local gossip was making a mountain out of a molehill, and that the innocence in your eyes was real.'

A little gasp escaped her lips. So, in spite of everything she had done, in spite of what she had suffered, there had still been gossip. She realised, of course, that it was Julie the unknown well-wishers had been concerned about, and not one of them had probably mentioned a name. It would have been an awkward 'one of your girls' or 'your sister' and Dane assumed that they were referring to her. In many ways it was a natural assumption, she supposed wretchedly. Julie was too young to be suspected.

She felt sick suddenly. People had long memories. If Julie's reputation was already damaged because of her folly of two years ago, then it would be disastrous if any word of her pregnancy were to get out. Little wonder she wanted it to be kept quiet.

'Well?' His voice intruded harshly on her unwelcome reverie. 'Haven't you got anything to say.'

'Is there any point?' she countered huskily. 'May I go now, please?'

'Presently,' he said. 'But first I want your word, for what it's worth, that you'll leave James alone. I don't know what wiles you used to persuade Julie to leave you with him in Skipton, but . . .'

'If I told you, you wouldn't believe me,' she interrupted wearily. 'Very well, you have my word. James shall be shunned. Now are you satisfied?'

For a moment he was silent, then a mirthless little smile touched his lips.

'If I told you, you wouldn't believe me,' he mocked, his eyes searing her suddenly, seeming to strip away the cumbersome coverings of coat and sweater and skirt— reminding her all too potently that she had once lain naked in his arms. And she remembered too how she had wanted him, the passionate need he had kindled in her that was to turn all too soon to pain and fear and disillusion.

The last two years had been a wasteland for her. She had told herself that Dane's cold-blooded possession of her had killed for ever the wellspring of warmth and giving within her. She had used her sexuality, her allure like weapons to keep the world at bay, and she had succeeded.

But she knew now it had been a hollow success. She had behaved coolly, keeping her admirers and would-be lovers at arms' length not through any failing of hers, but because not one of them had been able to rouse in her the deep yearning that she had known for Dane, and that not even his distrust or his brutal treatment had been able to stifle.

That was what she had been trying to conceal from herself over the past sterile months—that no matter what had happened between them, what depth of bitterness divided them, she wanted him still with every fibre of passionate being that she possessed.

Oh God, she thought dazedly, if he touched me—if he kissed me.

She saw him move, take one quick stride towards her, then pause, his mouth twisting in self-contempt.

He said harshly, 'You asked if you might go. What are you waiting for?'

Her lips moved, silently framing the word, 'Nothing'.

Then she turned and left him.

CHAPTER EIGHT

THAT evening Lisa came as near to quarrelling with Julie as she had ever done.

'Whatever possessed you to do such a thing?' she stormed at her. 'You made me look an utter fool—and worse. And what was this supposed appointment you had with the Vicar?'

Julie shrugged. She was sitting at her dressing table, brushing her hair, and she flicked Lisa a glance, her eyes suddenly wary.

'Just some problem over the hymns,' she said airily.

'Hymns?' Lisa stared at her. 'I thought it was the flowers.'

'Those as well. You know what these little country parishes are like. It takes ages for things to be arranged.' Julie's voice was placatory now, but Lisa was not to be so easily mollified.

'And you couldn't have waited five minutes for me?' she demanded.

'I was late,' Julie pleaded. 'And James didn't mind, I'm sure.'

'I minded,' Lisa told her frankly. And so did Dane, she thought. 'Did you get everything sorted out at the church?'

Julie fidgeted with her hairbrush. 'Not exactly. The Vicar was out on a sick call, so it was all rather a waste of time.'

'For God's sake, Julie,' Lisa sighed tiredly, 'what are you trying to do? I don't believe you were going to see the Vicar at all.'

There was a pause, then Julie said mutinously, 'All right—I wasn't. The truth is that James annoyed me, and

I just got in the car and drove off in a temper. I—I didn't really give you a thought until I was nearly halfway home, and it seemed pointless to come back. I knew James would offer to bring you.'

'Well, thanks on all counts,' Lisa said drily. 'What on earth did he say to you to provoke a reaction like that?'

Julie applied perfume to her pulse points. 'Nothing very much.' She gave a little unsteady laugh. 'I think it must be my condition. I seem to have a lower boiling point than usual. And James can be very aggravating.'

'I won't argue, because I don't know him that well,' Lisa tried to speak lightly, but inwardly she felt oddly uneasy although she couldn't define the reason for this. 'Is Tony coming to dinner tonight?'

'No,' Julie returned almost offhandedly. 'They have some relatives visiting, so he has to help entertain them.'

Lisa was a little surprised. 'Didn't he want you to be there?'

'Yes, he did as a matter of fact,' Julie said tartly. 'But I refused. I shall have to see quite enough of his far-flung family after we're married. I don't see why I should have to start now.' She swung round off her stool, giving Lisa a brilliant smile. 'Shall we go down? I love your dress. I wish I could wear that shade of green—it's such a subtle colour.'

She chattered about styles and shades all the way downstairs and into the drawing room where Chas was waiting for them. He was in high spirits, announcing that his physiotherapy seemed to be paying off at last.

'I may get back on the golf course, after all.' He beamed at them both, then looked at Julie. 'But I shan't be able to give you away, darling, not without a miracle. We'll have to resign ourselves to that. Unless you'd like to postpone the wedding for a few months,' he added with a chuckle.

'No!' Julie burst out almost violently. Her father looked

at her in swift surprise, and Dane who was standing at the other side of the room, pouring drinks, also glanced round, his brows raised. Julie forced a smile, leaning back in her chair, but Lisa saw that the knuckles on her clasped hands were white with strain. 'I—I'm sorry, Daddy.'

'It doesn't matter, darling,' Chas said mildly. 'I wasn't being serious, you know. I wouldn't stand in the way of young love. What a pity young Tony wasn't here to hear your impassioned cry. He'd have been most flattered!'

Julie murmured some constrained reply, and the moment passed.

As the wedding drew nearer, what had begun as a trickle of wedding presents developed into a flood. Julie might have insisted on a quiet ceremony with the minimum of fuss and number of guests, but there were still many people who wanted to remember her and wish her well

'I wish they wouldn't,' she said almost crossly one morning, surveying the latest additions. 'I'll never have room for all this stuff.'

'But you won't be spending your entire life in the flat,' Lisa pointed out. 'When you have a larger family, you'll need a house somewhere. A lot of these things can be stored until then.'

'Yes,' Julie said, and gave a slight shiver.

'What is it, love?' Lisa questioned.

'Oh—I was just thinking.' Julie gave an unconvincing little laugh. 'All the years ahead of me—actually being married to Tony. How strange it seems.' She saw Lisa regarding her worriedly, and smiled. 'I'm just being stupid, aren't I? Do you suppose all brides feel like this?'

'Perhaps,' said Lisa. 'I wouldn't know.'

'No.' Julie gave her a thoughtful look. 'Haven't you ever thought of getting married, Lisa? Being a top model, you must have met a lot of men. Surely there must have been someone you fancied.'

'Not enough for marriage,' Lisa said. Or for love, she added silently.

She smiled at Julie. 'Be content with your own wedding, ove. Don't try making matches for me. I'm perfectly happy as I am.'

The words made her cringe inwardly. Happy? Had she ever been less so? Even the frozen agony of humiliation and hurt which had driven her away from this place originally seemed in retrospect preferable to the limbo in which she now found herself.

She lay awake at night, gazing sightlessly into the darkness, praying for sleep to overtake her, but when it did, it was filled with feverish restless dreams.

The nights, she thought, were the worst. In the daytime she could keep busy, helping Julie unpack her wedding presents and list the donors, or walking round the grounds with Chas. The weather had taken an unseasonable spring-like turn. The snow showers and biting winds of the past weeks had vanished, and there was even an odd patch of snowdrops to be seen in a sheltered corner. But, as Chas said, it was probably too good to be true.

Dane she avoided as much as possible, a task made easier by his frequent absences. Chas grumbled goodnaturedly that they never saw anything of him these days, which led Lisa to suspect he was finding excuses to be away from the house. She told herself she ought to be grateful, when in reality she was crying inside.

But soon, soon, Julie would be married and then she could leave Stoniscliffe for ever, she told herself resolutely. Back in London her career was waiting for her. Even Simon was waiting for her. She had telephoned Jos to tell him when she expected to be back, and he had warned her that Simon had tried several times to find out where she was.

The Daltons had been to the house for dinner on several

occasions, and Lisa was immediately aware of a marked coolness in Celia's manner towards her. No doubt someone had told her that she'd been in James's car, she thought resignedly, and Celia was making her displeasure known.

But she certainly did not expect the next development. She was alone in the drawing room one afternoon when the door opened rather abruptly and Celia was shown in by a flustered-looking Mrs Arkwright.

'Oh.' Lisa put down the newspaper she'd been glancing at and got to her feet. 'Hello, Celia. Did you want to speak to Julie? She's not here at the moment. She . . .'

'I did not want to speak to Julie. My business is with you.' Celia snapped the words out, her eyes bright with anger.

'I don't think I understand,' Lisa said carefully.

'Oh, I'm sure you do.' Celia gave an unpleasant laugh. 'It's a pity there's no one here with a camera now. You could pose for a picture of guilt.' She walked aggressively up to Lisa and stood staring at her. 'Keep away from my husband!'

'Oh, come on,' Lisa exploded in her turn. 'I haven't seen him, except in your company.'

'Liar!' Celia's breathing was stormy. 'You've been with him, in his car when you were both supposed to be somewhere else. And you've been meeting him on the sly. I'm not a fool!'

Lisa controlled her temper with an effort. 'I'm sure you're not, but really, Celia, you're on the point of making an utter fool of yourself. James gave me a lift once, and once only. We really haven't the slightest interest in each other.'

'And you expect me to believe that?' Celia gave an incredulous laugh utterly devoid of mirth. 'Ever since you came back, James has been different—moody, restless, barely answering me civilly. And he can't even do his work properly. My father is furious.'

'Perhaps he's not well,' Lisa suggested temperately.

'Perhaps he's lovesick,' Celia snapped. 'Of course he was flattered by your interest—he's a man when all's said and done. But don't imagine there's anything more in it than that. James is married to me, and he knows when he's well off. He won't leave me.'

Lisa was suddenly weary, and disgusted by the vulgarity of Celia's remarks. 'Are you really sure of that? I'd have thought your visit here today was a sign of insecurity rather than anything else.'

Celia's hand jerked up and administered a vicious slap across Lisa's cheek. Lisa recoiled with a little cry, as a grim voice behind them demanded, 'Exactly what is going on here?'

'Dane!' Celia swung to him, her hands outstretched. 'I'm sorry to have made a scene, but I cannot reason with this girl. She doesn't realise the harm she's doing to my marriage —to me. I came here this afternoon to appeal to her, to try and make her see the damage her thoughtlessness is doing—and I'm afraid I lost my temper.'

Dane's voice became gentler. He said, 'I suggest you go home, Celia. You're doing no good here. I'll deal with Lisa myself.'

He escorted her to the door, and they disappeared. Presently Lisa, still standing rigidly by the sofa, heard the sound of Celia's car drawing away.

By the time Dane returned she was almost molten with rage.

'Before you say a word,' she said between gritted teeth, 'I am not, nor have I ever been having an affair with James Dalton. If he is carrying on with another woman, and God knows I wouldn't blame him, then his charming wife can look elsewhere for the culprit. It—is—not—me.'

'You little fool!' His voice bit at her. 'Didn't I warn you about Celia—about her obsessive jealousy? God knows you've done everything you can to add fuel to the flames—

talking about your girlhood crush on Dalton, accepting lifts in his car.'

She wanted to protest. After all, it wasn't her who had mentioned her crush, but Julie—and Julie had forced her into the position of having to come home with James. She wanted to say so, but something held her silent, some tiny flicker of unease.

Meanwhile Dane went on relentlessly, 'You'd better thank your lucky stars she only slapped you. It wouldn't have done your face much good if she'd used her nails, as she's quite capable of doing.'

Lisa felt a swift rush of nausea. She kept seeing Celia's face contorted with jealousy and rage, hearing her voice raised shrewishly, and for a moment she swayed a little, her hand raised to her burning cheek.

'Lisa!' Dane's voice sharpened into something like concern.

'I'm all right,' she said in a low voice. 'Just let me sit down for a moment.'

He swore under his breath, then moving as swiftly as a tiger stalking his prey, he lifted her into his arms and placed her on the sofa.

She stiffened in panic. 'Leave me alone!'

'Be quiet!' His voice was terse. 'I'll get you some brandy.'

'I hate brandy.' She found she was crying. Enormous tears she was unable to control were rolling down her pale cheeks. 'Just leave me alone—please. Oh, why did you ever have to bring me back here? I wish I'd died first!'

Dane's voice was harsh. 'And I? What do you imagine I feel? Don't you think I haven't cursed the day you came here? Do you think I haven't wished the past to be dead and buried a thousand times? But it isn't that easy, Lisa.' His voice sank almost to a whisper. 'You're like a madness inside me, a fever I can't cure.' He put out a hand, twining his fingers in her hair, examining the silky strands as if they were some exotic fabric, altogether foreign to his experience. Then his gaze shifted, resting almost tormentedly on her parted lips. He spoke hoarsely, his voice scarcely recognisable. 'Dear God, Lisa, give me back my peace of mind!'

He leaned forward, and his mouth took hungry possession of hers, kissing her so deeply that it seemed he would drain her sweetness dry.

She tried to struggle, but her body was pinned to the softness of the cushions by the weight of his, and she was unable to move except to lift and mould herself more closely against him. His hands were cupping her face, his thumbs softly stroking the line of her jaw, the curve of her throat, and all desire to fight him was dissolving away under the mastery of his touch.

His lips left hers and began to kiss her skin in brief featherlight caresses which left her craving for more. He let his mouth brush hers, then moved to linger on the lobe of her ear and the small erratic pulse in her throat.

Lisa heard herself gasp. Her hands slid up convulsively to fasten at the back of his head and draw him urgently down to her. Nothing seemed to matter except this wild excitement that Dane was creating within her. The bitter sterility of the past months seemed to roll away, and she was a young girl again, just emerging from the chrysalis of childhood, experiencing her first taste of physical passion with a man she had begun to love with all the single-mindedness of her youthful heart.

The realisation of it dazed her. All her life she had been telling herself she hated him, it seemed. But it wasn't true. She knew that now. Oh, in the beginning she had resented him, his lordly attitude, but his good opinions had mattered to her desperately. Even a casual word of praise had made her glow, and though they had been rare, she had treasured each one.

Even when she had joked with Julie over Dane's girl-friends, she had been aware of this strange, poignant ache deep within her.

She had told herself that she hated him, that his angry, contemptuous violation of her had withered the flowering of her womanhood, imposing a burden of frigidity upon her from which she could never recover. Every time another man had kissed her, tried to touch her, she had recoiled. And now she knew why.

As Dane's mouth gentled hers, as his hands stroked her body, her instinct carried her blindly towards passionate surrender. This was the power he had over her—that even when she had been most wounded by him, she would still have crawled to his feet for a tender word, a caress. That was what she had fled from—the acknowledgement of her submission, of the longing for him which transcended everything.

She was kissing him in her turn now, her lips moving softly and feverishly along the high cheekbones, the hard line of his jaw. She could think now of that dark summer dawn with regret instead of bitterness, knowing how different, how glorious it could have been.

A faint moan escaped her as Dane's hands slid beneath the fine wool sweater she wore to find and release the catch on her bra. He touched her breasts as if they were flowers, and they swelled and blossomed under his questing fingers.

Her yearning for him was becoming an agony. She was moving restlessly against him, her fingers tangling in his thick hair, tasting him, breathing him, longing to enfold him in the closest embrace of all.

Suddenly he groaned 'No!' against her mouth and levered himself up, away from her. There was a glazed, burning look in his eyes as he stared down at her, and strands of hair curled damply on his forehead. Lisa looked back at him, letting him read her own deep desires in her half-closed eyes, her languorous body and the softness of her trembling mouth.

She whispered longingly, 'Dane,' and he shook his head almost violently, jerking away from her so that he was sitting at the other end of the sofa, not touching her.

He muttered, 'Oh God, Lisa, what are we doing? We must be mad!' He looked around him, his mouth curling in self-derision. 'My father's drawing room,' he said flatly. 'Anyone could walk in at any time, yet you make me forget everything—even my sense of decency.'

She sat up stiffly, trying to push her sweater back into the waistband of her skirt with hands that shook too much to allow her to accomplish this simple task.

He said roughly, 'Let me.'

Lisa sat with bent head while he refastened and straightened her clothes as if she had been a child again. His breath was warm on her neck, on her averted cheek, and she felt him lift the heavy fall of tawny hair in his hands and carry it to his lips, burying his face in its scented mass. She quivered, remembering how only days before he had recoiled from the accidental brush of her hair across his face as if it had been contamination. He kissed the uncovered nape of her neck, his lips slow and tantalising, and she turned with a shudder of passion, her mouth seeking his.

He murmured something under his breath, then bent and kissed her again, a long leisurely exploration of her mouth which had her clinging mindlessly to him.

When he released her her head fell back against his shoulder.

He said thickly, 'I must have you. We must have each other. You know that, don't you? You're in my blood, God help us both.' He pushed the soft cloud of hair back from her face and looked down into her eyes, his own gaze questing and intent. 'Come to me tonight, Lisa.'

She could not deny him or the clamour of her senses. So she said on a little sigh, 'Yes—oh, yes!'

Dane bent and brushed his mouth across hers in promise and possession, then he rose and went quickly out of the room.

Lisa lifted her hand and pressed it against her lips as if she could capture and hold there Dane's last kiss. She felt almost dazed. What had just happened between them seemed past belief, and now she needed time to think, to consider it.

She could hear voices approaching the drawing room and she rose quickly and went over to the french windows, letting herself out into the cold air. It was late afternoon and already nearly dark, and a few flakes of snow drifted in the air, and Lisa went down the terrace steps on to the gravelled walk that traversed the house, uncaring of the cold.

She'd had to escape, she thought. She couldn't face anyone, take part in any normal conversation when her emotions were in such a turmoil.

Julie was probably too absorbed in her own affairs to pay much attention, but Chas would notice that she was distraite, she thought, lifting her hands and pressing them against her flushed cheeks.

It had occurred to her by now that Dane had not said one word of love. He had spoken of desire, of possession, of a fever in the blood, but that was all. She shivered suddenly, telling herself that it was the ice in the wind getting to her. She hugged her arms around her body and began to walk slowly round the house, keeping in its shelter.

Don't be a fool, she told herself harshly. It isn't a permanent relationship he's looking for. It's a cure for his fever. When the wedding is over and I'm back in London that will be the end of it.

But at least I'll have had tonight, and I can live on that for as long as I have to. Perhaps I'll be cured too, freed from these chains he's had round me since the first time I saw him. I can make a life for myself away from here, away from him. I've done it before. I'm a success.

And for him there'll be his work, this house and Tina or some other suitable lady.

She stopped at that, and stood staring unseeingly in front of her while the snowflakes clung to her face like frozen tears.

She went back into the house through the side door meaning to slip upstairs quietly to change for dinner, but the hall seemed unexpectedly crowded. Chas was there, looking handsome and leonine in one of his favourite velvet jackets, and Dane was standing behind him.

Lisa's heart missed a beat at the sight of him. She thought unsteadily, 'Oh God, I love him so!'

She wanted him to look at her, to smile, to share their secret knowledge that they would be together that night as lovers. But he didn't smile. His eyes as they met hers were as remote as a stranger's.

Julie started forward. 'Oh, there you are, darling. Lisa, you haven't been out in the snow without your coat? You'll have pneumonia for the wedding. No wonder I couldn't find you!'

'Have you been looking for me?' It was a stupid question, she thought, but what did it matter? All she really wanted to know was why Dane suddenly seemed a stranger again.

Julie laughed. 'All over the house. You've had a phone call—someone with a very sexy voice, called Simon. It seems he's missing you.'

Lisa stood very still. She said, 'But that's impossible! I didn't tell him where I was going.'

'Apparently he badgered the address from someone called Dinah. He said he knew you'd forgive him.' Julie laughed again. 'Well, darling, I think you might look a little more pleased. Isn't it nice to have a devoted swain pining for your return?'

Lisa didn't look at Dane. She said lightly, 'Fantastic. Now if you'll excuse me, I'll go up and change.'

'But aren't you going to phone him back?' Julie asked wonderingly.

Lisa's fingers tightened on the ornately carved banister rail. She said, 'Later, maybe,' and went upstairs without looking back.

When she was in her room, she reflected that Simon had obviously been giving Julie a line about how close they were. Clearly he'd been piqued by her sudden disappearance out of his life, and he couldn't have chosen a worse moment to force himself back into her notice. She smothered a sigh. Poor Simon, she thought ruefully. He would be even more piqued if he realised that she had barely given him a thought over the past days. He had no importance at all in her life and never would have, and this was something she would have to let him know as gently as possible when and if they met again.

She showered and changed as quickly as if she'd been getting ready for a modelling assignment, and made up with care before putting on a simple silky black dress with a full skirt of knife-edged pleats. She brushed her hair until it hung a glowing mass of colour on her shoulders, and put pearl studs in the lobes of her ears.

Tony had arrived when she went into the drawing room, and even a casual observer could have been certain that all was not well. He and Julie were standing together by the window engaged in a low-voiced but furious conversation. Tony looked angry and Julie mutinous, and Lisa's heart sank as she accepted a glass of sherry from Dane with a word of formal thanks. His duties as host accomplished, he turned away silently. Lisa stared after his tall figure as he moved across the room to speak to Chas. She tried to tell herself that his coldness was prompted by a desire for discretion, that later when they were alone he would be different. Her hands clenched into small tight fists in the folds of her skirt. Oh God, let it be true, she thought despairingly. She couldn't stand another rejection by him.

She went over to the windows and stood looking out into the darkness. It seemed to be snowing faster than ever. After a minute or two Julie joined her, her face flushed and her eyes ominously bright.

Lisa asked, 'What on earth's the matter?'

Julie gave a short, angry laugh. 'Not a great deal. Tony's miffed because some dreary carpet man was at the flat this afternoon, and I wasn't.'

Lisa gave her a swift glance. 'Did you know that he was going to be there?'

She shrugged. 'I forgot.'

'Oh, Julie!' Lisa sighed. 'How could you forget a thing like that?'

'Obviously quite easily,' Julie said flippantly. 'I do have other things on my mind apart from that blighted flat, but Tony, of course, takes it as a personal affront because his mother was there, having cancelled umpteen appointments, etcetera. Anyway, the carpets have been duly chosen, so I don't see what all the fuss is about.'

'Possibly over your lack of interest in your future home,' said Lisa, trying not to speak too sharply. 'Wouldn't it be better to tell Tony how you feel about the flat and see if there isn't some workable alternative?'

'If only there was,' Julie muttered, biting her lip.

Lisa, watching her surreptitiously during dinner, was worried to see that she and Tony were hardly speaking to each other, and that Tony had assumed an unattractively injured expression. It was hardly surprising that, just after Mrs Arkwright had brought coffee into the drawing room, Julie should abruptly announce that she had a headache and was going to bed, or that Tony should take his leave with a mumbled excuse only a few minutes later. Dane had already withdrawn to the study with his coffee to go over some papers, and Lisa found herself being inveigled into a game of chess with Chas.

He had taught her to play years before, and was proud of her prowess in the game, but tonight she was unable to concentrate and he found himself an easy victor. Seeing his evident disappointment, Lisa apologised and said that she was tired.

'Everyone's out of sorts this evening,' Chas grumbled, putting the chessmen away in their carved box. 'I hope you're not all sickening for the 'flu. And what was the trouble between Julie and Tony? Don't tell me he wasn't in a huff about something.'

'Oh, I don't think it was much.' Lisa tried to sound reassuring. 'It's a difficult time for them both. Julie's suffering from bridal nerves, I expect, and it's made her touchy.'

'Bridal nerves!' Chas scoffed. 'What on earth should she have those for? She's known Tony all her life. There won't be any major shocks in store. He's a good, dependable boy, and I never thought she'd have the sense to marry him.'

Lisa smiled and returned some neutral answer, but inwardly she was far from convinced that it was such an ideal match after all, and she wondered if Julie would still want to be married if she were not pregnant. Her indifference to, or even dislike of her future home, might be irrational in many ways, but then Tony's lack of sensitivity to her feelings about the situation was also disturbing.

When she went up to her room, she knocked gently on the adjoining door in case Julie was still awake and wanted to talk, but there was no answer.

She undressed slowly and put on her robe, not bothering

to switch on the light in her room. Then she sat down on the edge of her bed and waited. She heard Chas go to his room, and later the nurse bidding him goodnight. She sat and listened to the sounds of the house settling down for the night and her heart beat sounded slow and heavy in her ears as if she was part of some gigantic universal pulse. It seemed an eternity before everything was quiet and at last she moved. Her legs were shaking as she stood up. She went over to Julie's door and spoke her stepsister's name in a low voice, but there was still only silence, and she turned and went as swiftly and silently as a ghost out of her own door and down the passage.

Everywhere was darkness and shadows, and it was so quiet she thought she could hear the sound of the snow brushing the window panes.

When she reached Dane's door she stopped, trying to steady the swift panic of her breathing as her memories flooded back to haunt her.

But this time it would be different, she thought passionately. He didn't love her, but at least he didn't hate her either, and she would settle for that and what happiness she could snatch.

Noiselessly, she turned the handle and went into his room. It was dark, but there was sufficient light coming through the uncurtained window to show her that the wide bed was empty. Nor had it been occupied at any time that night. The covers were turned down neatly in Mrs Arkwright's inimitable fashion, and the pillow retained their pristine smoothness.

For a long minute she stood as still as a stone, then her hand crept up and touched her cheek as though someone had slapped her there and she was trying to soothe away the hurt of it.

She said, 'Dane,' and it came out on a small breath sounding like a sigh.

She went out of the room and down the gallery to the stairs. When she reached the hall, she could see a thin line of light showing under the study door, and she flung open the door and went in without knocking.

The desk lamp was lit and there were papers littered over the smoothly polished surface, but he wasn't working. He was leaning back in the chair, his jacket and tie discarded, and his shirt unbuttoned almost to the waist, the sleeves carelessly rolled up to reveal the strong muscular fore-arms. His dark hair hung untidily over his forehead as he stared down into the glass in his hand, and a half empty whisky decanter was stationed in front of him.

He said very quietly, 'What is it, Lisa?'

She didn't answer him at once, but stood staring at him unbelievingly. He swallowed the whisky in the glass he was holding and refilled it.

He repeated, 'What is it, Lisa? Did you want something?'

'I went to your room.' She spread her hands out in front of her in a little gesture of pleading. 'You weren't there—so I came to find you.'

'May I ask why?' He still hadn't looked at her. His voice was smooth and somehow remote as if he was more absorbed in his thoughts than their conversation.

She said heatedly, 'You know why. You asked me to come to you, so I'm here.'

'Indeed you are,' he said slowly. 'Yet I'd have thought your own common sense would have told you that my rather reckless invitation of this afternoon had been superseded by —other events, and that I neither need nor require your presence here or in my bed.'

She flinched. 'But why?' she whispered. 'Why are you doing this to me—to both of us?'

'For a number of reasons.' He lifted one shoulder in a weary shrug. 'I won't bother you with all of them, so let's just say that I could be acting out of misplaced consideration

for that poor fool waiting anxiously for you in London.
Presumably he thinks you're worth waiting for, so perhaps you hadn't better disillusion him too much.'

'Simon—you mean Simon?' She hadn't even given his unexpected phone call another thought. 'But he means nothing
to me . . .'

'He must mean something if you're currently sharing
your life with him,' he said flatly.

'My life?' she began incredulously, and then paused,
remembering how she had deliberately given him the impression that she and Simon were living together. She
swallowed. 'Oh, I see.'

'I'm glad you do.' Dane tipped his chair and stared at
her through half closed eyes. His mouth twisted derisively.
'You've a lovely face, Lisa, and a tempting body, but it's all
a façade. There's nothing behind your eyes and smile—no
loyalty, no womanliness, no warmth. Is that why you
waste yourself on casual encounters, because you know you
haven't sufficient depth in your nature to have a real relationship with a man? Why not break out of this mould
you've made for yourself? If this Simon loves you . . .'

'He doesn't,' she interrupted quietly. 'And nor do I love
him. As you say, it's completely casual.'

But not in the way you think, she added silently, her
heart wretched. Never in the way you think.

She said in a low voice, 'Dane, as soon as the wedding's
over I'll be gone, and you need never see me again.'

'I'm well aware of that, believe me,' he said harshly, and
she shrank a little. She had to rally her courage before she
could go on.

She said, 'I know you've always had a low opinion of me.
You never wanted me as a member of your family—or my
mother either.'

'Your mother I learned to accept.' He set the glass down
on the desk with such a thud that some of the amber

liquid it contained splashed out on to the desk top.

'You've spilled it—it will mark the wood.' Lisa glanced around her. 'Are there any tissues—a cloth perhaps?'

'Trying to convince me of your domestic virtues?' he jeered. 'It won't wash, Lisa, so just keep your distance—and fasten your robe,' he added with an edge to his voice. 'It seems to be slipping.'

Her face flaming, she obeyed.

'There's nothing wrong with my memory,' he continued after a pause. 'I can recall exactly what you look like naked. It's an image I've carried with me for two years, God help me. So I don't need any teasing glimpses. Save them and any other cheap tricks you have for the camera and your photographer boy-friend. Together you should be able to exploit a whole new market, Amber Girl.'

She folded her arms tightly across in front of her as if she was shielding herself from the contempt in his words.

His voice went on mercilessly. 'You spoke of your mother just now. What would Jennifer have thought if she could have seen some of the pictures of you splashed all over the glossy magazines? That gold mesh bikini which almost covered you, for instance. What would she have said if she'd seen her little girl, her pride and joy, displayed in that for all the world to leer over? Mightn't she have wondered where you got that trick of moistening your lips and looking at the camera as if you were offering Paradise in your eyes?'

She said, whispering, 'I was looking at you, Dane.'

'At me?' He gave a savage laugh. 'And why should that be, Lisa? What makes me so memorable among so many?'

Sudden bitterness entered her voice. 'Isn't it tradition—to remember the first man who made love to you. My God, love!' She threw back her head and stared at him. 'You talked about my mother, and what she'd think of my life as a model. What would she have thought of you, Dane, if she'd lived and found out that you'd raped me?'

'Good thinking, Lisa,' he said sardonically. 'But not convincing. That vicious little swine Laurie Hammond never bothered with a virgin in his life, and those parties he gave were notorious. If the drugs squad hadn't raided the house, I think a few local people were prepared to take the law into their own hands. And after being mixed up with a bastard like him, you dare to stand there and pretend your innocence!'

'Who told you that I was mixed up with him?' she asked raggedly. 'Gossip, rumour and innuendo. But I'll swear no one ever actually mentioned my name. No one said to you that Lisa Grayson was at one of the Hammonds' parties, did they, Dane, because they couldn't. Because I was never there, except for one afternoon when I walked over to the house to warn them . . .' She stopped, aware that she was on dangerous ground.

'Warn them of what? That a drugs raid was imminent? That a local lynch mob was being formed?'

She shrugged desperately. 'That they were becoming, as you said, notorious.'

'How very public-spirited of you,' he jeered. 'Am I really supposed to believe this fairytale?'

Lisa moved her hands wearily. 'Does it matter? Whatever story I told, you'd rather believe the worst of me. should be used to it by now.' She laughed wildly. 'God how I should be used to it! What a fool I was to think things could ever be different!'

'An unrealistic viewpoint, certainly.' Dane finished the whisky in his glass. 'Even if I'd taken you tonight, sooner or later Simon or someone else would have intervened, and I've no intention of turning myself into another scalp for you to hang on your predatory little belt, my sweet.'

'Do be careful, darling.' It was her turn to jeer. 'That sounds dangerously like an admission of weakness.'

'If it is,' he said quietly, and his eyes held hers for a

endless moment, 'then I'm managing to overcome it, thank you. Now perhaps you'd like to go back to your own room, and tomorrow we'll go on as usual, and pretend that little piece of madness this afternoon never happened.'

'As simple as that?' Lisa smiled crookedly. 'How nice for you! But I can't forget quite so easily. In fact, I've been fighting my memories tooth and nail for the past two years. I can't fight any longer. I—want you, Dane.'

As she spoke, her hands moved untying the sash of her robe and pushing it from her shoulders. It fell to the carpet around her feet, and she looked at him with her heart in her eyes, desiring him totally, mutely begging him to desire her in return.

He didn't move. He was so still, he might have been carved out of stone. He said thickly, 'Of course it isn't as simple as that. If I said I wasn't tempted, I'd either be a saint or a liar, and I've never been a saint, as you have good reason to know. But it's a question of priorities, and yours, such as they are, are elsewhere. Now cover yourself, and get out of here.'

For a moment Lisa still stood there, unable to accept that once again she had failed. It was almost ludicrous, she thought dazedly. She knew without conceit the effect she had on most men who looked at her. There was hunger in Simon's face each time she walked across the room, although he kept it under a tight rein. And yet she could stand here in front of Dane, naked, and it made no difference. He was turning her away again.

She bent swiftly and retrieved her robe, fastening it round herself with grace and a kind of pathetic dignity as she strove silently to master her emotions.

Dane got to his feet. 'For God's sake, go!' There was an edge to his voice. His control was shaken and she knew it, but it had not broken and there was nothing for her here but rejection, as it seemed there had always been.

Silently Lisa turned and left the room. She felt numb as she climbed the stairs, except for a tightness in her throat, and a hot burning sensation behind her eyes. But she was not going to let herself cry. She'd shed too many tears already.

Later, she thought detachedly, she would probably feel ashamed at the way she had offered herself. But not now.

All she could think of now was flight, away from this place and away from this man for ever.

CHAPTER NINE

LISA went into the darkness of her room and stood there, trying to collect together the thoughts that seemed to be buzzing aimlessly in her brain, and which she needed to channel into some kind of decisive action.

But what? she thought. It was impossible for her to leave now. She would have to wait for daylight at least and make her way to Leeds for the first available train to London. She would have to think of some story that would satisfy Chas, and she would have to tell Julie that she could not stay for the wedding—find some convincing explanation for her absence. Not the truth, of course. That was also impossible.

When she heard the sound of the muffled sob for one crazy reeling moment she thought it came from her own throat, and she put a hand over her mouth, desperately damming back any further sound.

And then she realised that it came from the adjoining room. She stiffened, listening intently. It was probably nothing, she tried to tell herself. A bad dream perhaps. People sometimes cried out in bad dreams. But even as she listened the sound of Julie's weeping became louder and more persistent.

Some of the rigidity left Lisa and a deep sigh welled up inside her, even a flicker of resentment. She was desperately unhappy, yet it was Julie who was crying in the night, and she would have to go to her as she had done ever since they were children together, and soothe her and bring her calm and what comfort she could.

The bedside lamp was on in Julie's room and Julie was

lying across the bed, her body shaking, her face half hidden in the pillow. Lisa sat down on the bed and placed a tentative hand on her shoulder, realising with brief amazement that Julie was fully dressed.

She said gently past the pain in her throat, 'Darling—what is it? Please tell me.'

'I can't.' There was a moan in Julie's muffled voice. 'I can't tell anyone.'

Lisa sighed again. 'And you can't go on forever carrying this burden of secrecy of yours. What is it?' She paused, remembering the subdued anger on Tony's face before dinner, the stormy feeling in the air. 'Have you quarrelled?'

There was a silence, and then Julie sat up, flinging her arms round Lisa and putting her wet face down on her shoulder.

'Yes,' she wailed, her slim body shaking again. 'Yes—and, oh Lisa, I can't bear it! I'm never going to see him again.'

Lisa bit her lip. 'Julie love, these things happen in the weeks before a wedding. I'm sure it isn't anything really serious. I could see you weren't on the best of terms, but . . .'

'It's true,' Julie insisted almost hysterically. 'He told me that we mustn't meet any more. He said it was madness. I—I nearly told him about the baby. I wanted to tell him, but I couldn't find the words.'

'Do you want me to tell him for you?'

There was a pause and then Julie shook her head. 'No,' she said dully.

'But he can't just escape all his responsibilities like this,' Lisa said sharply. 'The wedding is so soon. What are his family going to think?'

'His family?' Julie gave a little cracked laugh. 'You mean the Bainbridges, don't you? You think I'm talking about Tony?'

'Of course.' Lisa felt cold suddenly, as if a hitherto

confusing pattern had suddenly taken on a recognisable and frightening shape. 'Isn't this what you're telling me? That you've quarrelled with Tony?'

Julie shook her head slowly. Her eyes drowned in tears looked into Lisa's.

'It's James,' she said on a little catch of the breath. 'James Dalton. I've loved him for over a year. But she'll never let him go. He belongs to her, just one of the possessions her father's money has bought. He hasn't anything of his own. Even the house is in her name only.' The words seemed to tumble out of her as Lisa listened, stricken. 'He doesn't love her. She treats him like dirt. She even blames him for the fact that they haven't any children—she says it's his fault. But she's wrong.'

'Oh God,' Lisa muttered. She swallowed. 'Julie, are you trying to tell me that James is the baby's father?'

'Yes,' Julie said simply with a certain pride.

'But Tony—where does he figure in all this?' Lisa demanded almost wildly.

Julie gave a defensive shrug. 'He wanted to marry me. I couldn't have James, and I needed someone to look after me.'

'But you can't do this,' Lisa said urgently. 'Didn't your own sense of decency—of morality—tell you that you can't marry one man to provide you with a ready-made father for someone else's child?'

'But Tony wants to marry me.' Julie's face had relapsed into a sullen scowl. 'He was always hanging round. He's happy, so why should you make a fuss?'

'He didn't look very happy tonight.'

'Oh, that.' Julie shrugged again swiftly. 'That wasn't important. I'll just have to be nice to him, that's all. He'll soon come round.'

'So while you were supposed to be deciding on carpets, I suppose you were really having one of your assignations with James. And that also explains those early walks,' Lisa said grimly. 'May I enquire, just for the record, why you tried to thrust me at him?'

Julie thrust out her bottom lip. She looked very young and Lisa longed to box her ears.

'Celia was suspecting things. She was almost accusing James of having an affair—so . . .'

'So you thought you'd make me the target for her justifiable susicions,' Lisa supplied drily. 'Thank you so much! I don't envy you when she discovers the truth. She'll probably tear you apart.'

'You wouldn't tell her? Lisa—promise me . . .'

'I shan't say a word.' Lisa got to her feet. 'I'm leaving by the first train tomorrow anyway.'

'Because of this?' Julie stared up at her.

'For reasons of my own.'

'But you won't be here for the wedding.'

'Julie!' Lisa had turned to leave, but now she swung back on her stepsister. 'Are you quite mad? You can't intend to go through with this marriage. You couldn't do such a thing. You don't love Tony—that's been more than evident all along, even if I didn't want to believe it. You've made a fine mess of your own life, but you can't drag him into it. It wouldn't be fair.'

'But I've got to marry him!' Julie's voice held panic 'What about the baby? What could I do?'

Lisa groaned and sat down on the bed again, taking her stepsister's trembling hands into hers.

'You could start to control your own life instead of letting it control you,' she said, making her voice harsher than usual. 'You can't run and dodge and hide behind other people for ever. Besides, there's a practical point. Tony may be doting, but he isn't a fool. Unless you and he have been lovers, there is no way in which he'll accept that baby as his own, and from what you've been saying, gather that you haven't slept together. Have you?

Julie stared down, her lips mutinously folded. 'No,' she muttered at last. She was trembling and her fingers plucked convulsively at the pattern of the bedcover, pulling at the threads. 'Lisa, I'm so frightened! Please help me. What can I do?'

'You could come to London with me,' Lisa said reluctantly. 'There's room at the flat, although it would be a squash. And I could support you until the baby's born at least. Your father has been making me an allowance and I haven't touched it, not a penny. We could use that.'

'I can't,' Julie whispered, her eyes enormous. 'Everyone would find out, and I couldn't bear it.'

'You'll have to face up to it sooner or later,' Lisa returned wearily. 'Have you considered what will happen when James gets to hear of your pregnancy and does some calculations?'

'He won't,' said Julie, but her voice lacked conviction. 'But I can't call off the wedding, Lisa. You must see that. Daddy still hasn't fully recovered. The shock might make him ill again.'

Her voice had brightened a little, as if she had now justified herself, Lisa thought with a silent groan. Did Julie really think anything would be gained by protecting Charles from a small scandal now, when so much deeper trouble was waiting for them?

She made herself speak calmly. 'I can't argue with you any more, Julie. We'll talk again tomorrow before I go. Can I count on you to drive me to Leeds for the train?'

'Of course I will,' Julie assured her, then hesitated. 'But —but I won't come with you, Lisa. I just couldn't.

Lisa forced a smile. 'Then I won't say any more about it. But you must think about what I've said, Julie. You can't ruin people's lives in order to protect yourself.'

She lay in bed, but sleep was impossible. She made herself think about Julie because it made a barrier to the pain that she experienced each time she let herself think about Dane. There was a wellspring of agony inside her just waiting for an opportunity to release itself, and she couldn't allow it to happen. So instead she lay staring into the darkness and wondering why she hadn't guessed the truth about Julie when all the clues had been there.

Perhaps after all, her protectiveness towards her stepsister had been a disservice, she thought wretchedly. Instead of taking the blame on her own shoulders and suffering for it, perhaps it would have been better if she had told Dane that it was Julie who had been slipping away to the Hammonds' parties. She had intended to shield Julie from his anger and had brought it on herself.

It could all have been so different, she thought. Yet now Julie, the cherished and protected, seemed to think she was above the ordinary moral laws of society.

We've all handled her with kid gloves for too long, Lisa acknowledged to herself, watching dry-eyed a cold grey dawn lift the immediate darkness from her window.

As soon as it was light, she packed swiftly, folding away the clothes she had brought with mechanical neatness. It had stopped snowing in the night, but the landscape outside looked hostile and alien in its white shroud, and she bit her lip until it bled, worrying that perhaps she might not be able to get away after all. But the milkman called, and after him the newspapers and the mail van, and she relaxed. At least the roads were passable even if driving conditions were far from ideal.

She waited in her room until she saw Dane's car leave for the day, then she went downstairs and had a hurried breakfast of toast and coffee. When she had finished, she went to Chas's room. He was dressed and in his wheelchair, frowning over the crossword and accepting glumly the pills that the nurse was inexorably offering him. His face lit up when he saw Lisa.

'There you are, my pet. It looks as if Julie will have a white wedding in more ways than one.'

'Yes, doesn't it?' she said steadily. 'But it looks as if I'm going to have to miss it. I had a letter from my agent this morning. It's a job—a big one, and it won't wait. Unless I return to London today I may miss it.'

'Would that be so very terrible?' Chas looked wounded, and Lisa felt immediate guilt.

'It is my living,' she pointed out gently.

'I was going to talk to you about that,' Chas said quickly. 'You don't have to work for a living, Lisa. I can still support my family, thank God, in spite of the recession. And it's going to be lonely in the house with Julie gone. I hoped you'd stay.'

'I can't.' Her voice broke very slightly. 'I—I must go back to London. I don't belong here, Chas. I'm an outsider, and I always will be. I love you, and I'll always be grateful to you, but it's better for everyone if I go—you must believe that.'

The nurse had already tactfully left the room and Chas leaned forward, his face concerned.

'Darling girl, I don't want to pry, but it's Dane, isn't it? He can be tough, I know. Has he hurt you? I'll talk to him . . .'

'No—please.' Lisa braced herself against the pleading look in her stepfather's eyes. 'There's nothing anyone can say or do. We're just better apart, that's all. I should never have come back here.' She paused. 'I'm sorry.'

'And so am I,' Chas said gently. 'More sorry than I can say. But you have your own life to lead, Lisa, and I can't interfere in that. Do you really have to leave before the wedding? Julie—everyone—will be so upset.'

'I've already explained to Julie that I can't be there,' Lisa said quietly. 'I think she understands.' And I can't interfere in her life and tell you that there shouldn't be any wedding, she thought unhappily. Julie must do what seems best to her, and I can only pray she doesn't wreck too many lives.

When she returned to her bedroom, Julie was waiting for her.

'You were serious, weren't you?' She gestured towards Lisa's case. 'You're really leaving. Because of me?'

'Not entirely,' Lisa returned with deliberate evasiveness.

Julie looked at her with painful eagerness. 'You've said goodbye to Daddy? Did you—did you tell him?'

'No,' said Lisa, and sighed at the expression of relief on Julie's face. 'It's all right, Julie. Your secret as ever is safe with me.'

'You're an angel!' Julie planted a swift kiss on her cheek. 'It will all work out, Lisa, you see if it doesn't.'

'You have a great talent for self-deception,' Lisa said bitterly. 'But we won't discuss it any further. Do you want to risk driving me, or shall I phone for a taxi?'

'Oh, the snow's nothing,' Julie said negligently. She paused. 'Isn't there anyone else you want to say goodbye to?'

'No.' Lisa met her gaze squarely. 'No one.'

Julie shrugged. 'Then we may as well be on our way.' Her voice sounded nonchalant, but the look she sent Lisa was an uneasy one.

As they drove away from the house Lisa thought drily that for the first time in their lives Julie was probably relieved to see her go. She knew altogether too much.

They spoke in snatches as the car moved decorously along the snowy roads. Lisa was glad to see that Julie appeared to be concentrating on her driving, and taking fewer chances than on other occasions. It was a straight road, too, bordered on each side by dry stone walls and deep ditches. Beyond the walls, sheep huddled together, their fleeces brown and grey when seen against the dazzling whiteness around them.

As they waited at a 'Give Way' sign for another car to

complete its manoeuvre, Julie said suddenly, 'That's funny —there's Dane.'

'Where?' Lisa sat forward sharply, peering through the windscreen. 'It can't be. He went to the works. I saw him leave.'

'Perhaps he had to come back for something.' Before Lisa could say or do anything, Julie sounded her horn and waved. 'He's seen us,' she added with satisfaction.

Lisa smothered a groan. 'Don't stop,' she said urgently.

'What?' Julie glanced at her. 'But he's stopping. He obviously wants to speak to us.'

'Well, I don't want to speak to him. Julie, for God's sake drive on—please!' The emotion throbbed in Lisa's voice and Julie gave a puzzled sigh.

'Oh, very well. But he won't be too pleased.' She let in the clutch abruptly and the car jerked forward.

Lisa sat back in her seat, but Julie's next words had her twisting round anxiously. 'He's following us.'

'But that's ridiculous!'

'Do you want us to leave him behind? I can try if you like.' Julie accelerated and the little car shot forward.

'No, don't!' Lisa was appalled at the idea.

Julie looked in her mirror. 'He's flashing his lights. He wants us to stop.' She giggled. 'We'll give him a run for his money.'

She accelerated again and Lisa said sharply, 'Julie, slow down, for heaven's sake!'

'Why should I?' Julie demanded recklessly. 'After all, you were the one who didn't want to talk to him.'

'But we can't outrun him, even if the road was perfect.' Lisa watched the mounting speedometer needle with alarm.

'Oh, don't make such a fuss,' sighed Julie. 'It's only snowy. There isn't really any ice.'

As she spoke the car seemed to lurch and begin to slide

sideways. Lisa saw Julie, white-faced, wrench at the wheel
and tried to call a warning, but the word stuck in her
throat. She felt the car lift as they hit the verge and then
slide forward into the ditch. She felt something hit her
head, and then everything went dark.

There was a blur of light, and the sound of voices—urgent
voices but far in the distance. She tried to answer because
she thought she heard her name being called, but there was
no sound, as if her throat muscles would not obey her.
Eventually she seemed to croak something, and that seemed
to satisfy the voices, because they stopped, and she was
able to sleep.

She came awake slowly, aware of a throbbing pain in her
temple, and a more generalised ache throughout her body
and limbs. The first person she saw was Chas sitting beside
her. She was in bed in a strange room, obviously a side
ward in a hospital.

She smiled at him, using her facial muscles gingerly.

'I feel like a walking bruise,' she said.

Chas took her hand. 'You're going to feel like that for a
day or two,' he said. 'That damned car turned over.'

She had just been going to ask him what she was doing
there, but then it all came flooding back, and she bit back a
little cry.

'Julie—is Julie all right?'

'She's going to be fine,' he said heavily, after a pause, and
Lisa looked into his face and saw the knowledge there, and
the sorrow.

She said in a low voice, 'She's lost the baby, hasn't
she?'

'Yes.' His shoulders sagged defeatedly. 'I'm trying to tell
myself it's all for the best—under the circumstances. I only
wish I could believe it.' He hesitated. 'It's hit Tony hard,
damned hard. I've cancelled the wedding, naturally.

would probably have had to be postponed as it was, but there's no chance now of it ever taking place. He did offer to come and see her, but I could tell his heart wasn't in it, so I think they're best apart.'

Lisa said, 'I suppose so. I tried to tell her . . .'

'Did you know that Tony wasn't the father?' The sharpness in Chas's voice revealed the strain he was under.

'Yes, I knew. She told me.' Lisa waited for the next question, but it didn't come.

'I blame myself in many ways. She wasn't strong when she was a young child, and I always gave in to her more than I should have done.' He swallowed. 'If my Jennifer—if your mother had lived, she might have been different. Julie cared for her, cared for her opinion. As it was, we all protected her, made excuses for her, where I should have taken a firm line with her.' He shook his head almost wonderingly. 'But she would have deceived him—deceived that poor lad into marrying her. That's what I find so hard to take. She's behaved as if morality were only for other people.'

He needed to talk, Lisa knew, and the least she could do was listen, but when eventually Miss Henderson arrived to take him back to Stoniscliffe, her head was throbbing quite agonisingly.

The room to herself again, she lay back on her pillows and closed her eyes, as a few scalding tears trickled under her lashes and down her pale cheeks.

'Weeping for your ruined beauty?' Dane asked harshly.

Her eyes flew open, and her lips parted in a startled gasp as she looked up at him. How long had he been standing here watching her weep? she wondered.

Then his actual words penetrated her consciousness and he lifted a hand and touched the pad of dressing and the bandage on her forehead and winced.

'Don't look so petrified,' the grim voice went on. 'It's not a serious cut. They tell me there won't even be a scar. You've got off lightly again, Lisa.'

'Don't,' she whispered. 'Oh God, please don't!'

His hand gripped her wrist, bruising the flesh, and she gave a little cry.

'Just where did you think you were going this morning?' he asked coldly. 'How did you manage to persuade Julie to take you in those conditions? You know she isn't a wonderful driver at the best of times. But that wouldn't weigh with you, would it, Lisa? Running away is the only answer you have, and it didn't matter to you that you were risking not just your own life but my sister's as well.'

She closed her eyes against the hard, bitter light in his. He was blaming her for what had happened. He thought she had encouraged Julie to speed. She wanted to defend herself, to fling his words back in his face, but her head was aching too badly, and she felt too weak.

She said in a low voice, 'I didn't mean this to happen.'

'Oh, I give you credit for that. But there are some things you can't escape the responsibility for by pleading your good intentions, and my sister's life ruined is only one of them.'

'How am I supposed to be responsible for that?' She wanted to cradle her aching head in her hands, but knew he would interpret it as a ploy to gain sympathy.

'Whose example did she have to follow in her most impressionable years? Yours, Lisa, only yours. She thought the world of you, and always has done. Did she know about your association with Laurie Hammond? Did she think it was romantic perhaps? And these sordid associations of yours in London—did she find them glamorous? Oh, yes, Amber Girl, you set the example, only Julie wasn't quite as wise in the ways of the world, as able to avoid the consequences of her actions. You made an innocent girl think that sleeping around was fun.'

His words were like hammer blows striking her to the heart, and she reeled back under them.

'Julie's life is in pieces around her, and you've escaped with a slight scratch. The pattern just repeats itself endlessly. I realise now why she was so desperate to have you here, why you were the only one who would do. Because you'd know what to do, wouldn't you, Lisa, you'd be able to find a way out of this mess she was in—perhaps even recommend a good abortion clinic where they wouldn't ask too many questions. But your advice was different, wasn't it? You told her to go on with this charade of a wedding, and take the unfortunate Bainbridges for everything they'd got.'

'No,' she uttered faintly. Her mouth was burningly, bitterly dry, and there were small coloured lights dancing meaninglessly in front of her eyes. Dane seemed to loom over her, the anger and darkness within him striking at her soul's core. She fumbled for the buzzer switch beside the bed, but there was no strength in her fingers, and the darkness was crowding around her again, only this time she almost welcomed it. As it was, the last thing she saw was the bitterness in Dane's eyes before she fell, silently screaming, into the abyss.

She was dimly aware of noise, of bustle, and the small sharp pain of an injection in her arm, and she subsided gratefully into the peace of a drugged sleep.

It was daylight when she opened her eyes, a bright cold day with a brilliant blue sky, and a sharp sun glittering on the snow-covered rooftops she could see from the window. Almost as if there had been some prearranged signal, the door opened and a nurse came in carrying a washbowl and a towel.

'Feeling better today, are we?' she asked breezily. Dr Simms says you're to stay with us for a couple more days for observation after last night's little do. And you're not to have visitors if they're going to upset you.'

A reluctant smile touched Lisa's lips as she heard the note of admonishment.

She said, 'You can leave me the bowl. I can manage for myself.'

'Well, if you're sure.' The young nurse cast a harassed glance at her watch. 'It will be time for rounds, and we're all behind today. Someone will be along presently to change your dressing.'

She whisked out again, leaving Lisa to enjoy the refreshment of a leisurely wash. Her head was only aching slightly today, and she felt more comfortable generally.

The real hurt was within, deep and savage, as Dane's words came accusingly back at her. Always and always he would believe the worst, and always the evidence would condemn her.

It hadn't merely been his own anger which had made him speak so cruelly to her, she thought tiredly. His behaviour had also been prompted by his anxiety and concern for Julie, and she could understand that.

She thought, 'He loves Julie. He cares about her.' And somehow that realisation only made the inner pain worse. Because once, for a brief ephemeral time, Dane might have loved her too. Once his awakening desire might have been transmuted into something deeper, and more tender.

She knew now that she hadn't only been shielding Julie in those days, but Dane as well from the pain of disillusion from the young sister he loved. Both Chas and he would have been hurt by the truth, so she had remained silent and through that silence she had been the one to suffer.

Flowers arrived during the course of the morning from Chas of course, and a nurse told her that there had been numerous phone calls asking after her, some of them from newspapers.

Lisa groaned inwardly. She had forgotten that the Amber

Girl was still news, and was glad that the strict hospital rules protected her from any enterprising reporter's invasion.

She found she was behaving with total docility, resting when she was told, eating the meals brought to her with a complete lack of appetite.

Dr Simms was pleased with her and said so on his evening visit. If she continued to make progress she could go home the day after tomorrow. He was less pleased when Lisa told him she would be returning to London as soon as she left hospital.

'I don't care for that idea at all,' he said flatly. 'You've had a bad shock, and a nasty bump on the head, and you need to rest in an environment where you'll be looked after, at least for a week. I'll have a word with your stepfather.'

Lisa didn't argue any more, but her mind was made up. There was no way she was going back to Stoniscliffe, no matter what pressure the doctor or Chas brought to bear.

To change the subject, she asked how Julie was getting on. She'd asked at intervals during the day, and had been told that her stepsister was as well as could be expected but under sedation.

Dr Simms frowned a little. 'Physically, she's comfortable, but she doesn't help herself. She's in a highly emotional state, and we're having great difficulty with her—trying to help her to calm down and accept what has happened.' He hesitated. 'I did hope that her fiancé could be of assistance, but the very idea made her so hysterical that we couldn't pursue it.'

Lisa bit her lip. 'I think the engagement is at an end,' she ventured, wondering how much Julie had let slip in the presence of the medical staff.

'I see.' Dr Simms looked rather disapproving.

'Perhaps I could see Miss Riderwood,' Lisa suggested, but the doctor shook his head.

'She's asleep a great deal of the time, and apart from that we've been instructed that only her immediate family are allowed to visit. Her father is coming again this evening.'

Lisa was silent. She didn't even have to ask who had issued such instructions. She knew only too well.

The morning papers were something of a shock. In most of them, Lisa learned, she was seriously injured, even disfigured for life.

'What nonsense!' one of the nurses snorted as she changed Lisa's dressing with deft fingers. 'Why, this little cut won't even leave a mark. Do they think we don't know how to look after you?'

Lisa wearily realised there was an edge of resentment in the nurse's voice, as if she herself was responsible for the inventions in the papers—she who had seen no one and made no telephone calls. Or perhaps I'm just being over-sensitive, she thought.

But she didn't think so. There was little doubt that all the staff now knew of Dane's ruling that she was not to see Julie, and had speculated as to the cause. Lurid newspaper stories wouldn't do her cause any good at all.

She was dozing after lunch when a slight sound aroused her and opening her eyes, she saw with amazement that James Dalton was standing beside her bed. He was carrying a bunch of flowers, which he proffered awkwardly.

'I'm sorry,' he said. 'They didn't tell me at the office that you were asleep.'

'They probably didn't know.' Lisa sat up, trying to smile. 'I—I feel rather a fraud, lying here in bed, when there's nothing really the matter with me.'

James made some stilted reply, then brought one of the chairs forward and sat down beside the bed. There was an expression of strain on his face.

After a pause, Lisa said with slight reserve, 'It's very

kind of you to come to see me, James, but I don't think
Celia . . .'

'To hell with Celia!' he interrupted with sudden controlled violence. 'I had to come, Lisa. I have to know the
truth. There are so many rumours buzzing round, and I've
got to pretend to stand aloof—not to care when I'm almost
going out of my mind.' He looked at her with agony in his
eyes. 'Is it true that Julie had a miscarriage?'

Lisa nodded slowly, and his breath escaped in a deep
groan.

He said huskily, 'Oh God—was it my child? Did she
ever say anything to you—about us?'

'She did confide in me—just before the accident,'
Lisa said cautiously. 'She was rather upset. She said there'd
been a quarrel.' She hesitated.

'Yes, we'd quarrelled.' James gave a mirthless laugh. 'I
tried to tell her that we must stop seeing each other—that
her marriage was going to change everything, of necessity.
She seemed to think that our relationship could just continue as it always had done. I knew she didn't love Bainbridge, and I tried to persuade her not to go through with
it.'

'Why?' Lisa asked coolly. 'So that you, a married man,
could keep Julie for your exclusive benefit? How nice for
her!'

James winced. 'Yes—I suppose that was what I meant,
even if I wasn't prepared to admit it. But I love her, Lisa.
We love each other. She's my reason for living. I knew
Bainbridge wasn't her lover, and then when I heard this
rumour about the baby, and the engagement being off,
everything seemed to fall into place. I knew I wouldn't be
allowed to see her. I had to be careful in making enquiries
unless it got back to Celia . . .'

'Oh, we must be careful for none of this to get back to
Celia,' Lisa said scornfully. 'How are you going to explain

your visit to me, may I ask?'

James shrugged helplessly. 'That, I don't know.' He paused. 'I know you despise me, Lisa. I can see it in your face. But I swear I had no idea that she was expecting my child.'

'Would it have made any difference?' Lisa asked quietly. 'You're still very much married to Celia.'

'I don't know,' James said wretchedly. 'But I know that the loss of the baby has made a world of difference. That's a paradox, isn't it, but it's true. Julie and I belong together, and never more so than now. I should have the right to be with her, to comfort her. I need that right, and by God, I'm going to have it.'

Lisa stared at him. 'You mean you'd be prepared to leave Celia—give up the good life?' she asked rather cynically, and he flushed.

'The only good thing in my life has been Julie. I let myself be dependent on Celia because I didn't really care what happened to me. But I could make out on my own. I was happy when we were in Africa. I had a job there I was good at.' His lips tightened. 'Celia wasn't in control then. I think that's why she insisted on coming home, rather than the threat of some non-existent revolution, because she wanted to have the whip hand as she'd always been used to. Well, she's wielded that whip for the last time. If she won't agree to a divorce, then we'll wait and obtain one without her consent. There's no reason for anyone to be tied to a failed marriage these days.'

Lisa gave him a long look. There was no doubting his sincerity, but why hadn't he thought of this at the beginning of their affair? It was probably significant that it was the loss of the baby that had made him contemplate the destruction of his secure existence as Celia's husband. Hadn't Julie said that Celia had taunted him over their own child-lessness, blaming him for it? Might it not be Julie proving

Celia wrong once and for all which had tipped the scales in her favour? If so, this was a fragile foundation for their future happiness.

But that, Lisa told herself, is none of my business. There'll be one hell of a row, but they have their own lives to lead. Surely they can't make much more of a mess of them than they have done already.

James leaned forward and took her hand. He said urgently, 'Lisa, listen to me, can you get along to see Julie. Can you give her a message?'

Lisa shook her head. 'It's impossible. I'm not allowed to see Julie. You see, she was driving me to Leeds to catch a train when the accident happened, and they think I'm to blame . . .'

'They think?' James gave her an incredulous look. 'I can't believe Charles Riderwood could be such a fool. The worst anyone could say about you is that you were reckless to have hitched a ride with her, because she must be the world's worst driver.'

Lisa bent her head. 'Nevertheless there's an embargo on my seeing her.'

James's face was dismayed. 'Then what am I going to do?' he muttered, half to himself.

'I'm sure you'll think of something,' Lisa assured him drily. 'The pair of you have managed quite well up to now.'

'Yes.' James seemed oblivious to the sarcastic note in her voice. 'Perhaps if I wrote a note, I could ask one of the nurses to give it to her.' He paused and looked at Lisa. 'You still think I'm a pretty poor specimen, don't you, but I'll make it all up to her, Lisa, I swear I will.' His voice broke suddenly, and he bent forward, burying his face in the crisp coverlet. He said, 'I've never felt like this before about anyone. You must believe me.'

Lisa looked down at his ruffled fair head with a faint despair. She touched his hair tentatively.

'I believe you,' she said gently.

It was the faintest sound—no more than an indrawn breath—that alerted her to the fact that they were not alone. She glanced up, startled. The door to her room stood open, and Dane was standing there as if frozen.

Over James's bent head, their eyes met, hers with a kind of defiant pleading, his bleak with incredulity and contempt.

Then as silently as he had appeared, he was gone, the door closed between them with total finality.

CHAPTER TEN

'A NICE kettle of fish this has turned out to be!' Myra said accusingly. She and Jos sat on either side of Lisa's bed, their faces full of affectionate concern, and gradually the deep chill inside Lisa began to thaw.

'It's so wonderful to see you both—such a surprise,' she said.

'Not half as much of a surprise as I got when I opened the papers this morning,' Jos said grimly. 'I telephoned the hospital at once. Didn't they give you my message?'

Lisa shook her head. 'I don't really think I'm their favourite patient at the moment. I'm here because this is a private ward, and my stepfather's paying for me to be looked after, but they think I'm a perfectly well lady with a gift for self-dramatisation.'

'Cheek!' Myra said indignantly. She gave the strip of sticking plaster adorning Lisa's forehead an anxious look. 'What's underneath that?'

'Not a lot,' Lisa assured her, her lips widening into her first genuine smile.

'Thank God for that,' Myra said promptly, and sat back.

'What a great diplomat the world lost in you, darling,' Jos gibed. He smiled at Lisa. 'There'll be no permanent damage. I suppose they've told you that.'

'Oh, yes—Dr Simms has been very reassuring. I just wish I could care more,' Lisa said with a brief sigh.

'Hey!' Jos ran a finger down her cheek. 'We'll do the caring. You just concentrate on getting well. You're one of my meal tickets, remember.'

'One of the many,' Lisa countered, and they grinned at

173

each other with understanding.

Myra was looking around, her nose wrinkled. 'Hospitals all smell the same. How long do you have to stay here?'

'I don't.' Lisa shook her head. 'I think they'd be quite glad to see the back of me.' She hesitated. 'Can I come back to London with you?'

'Of course,' Jos and Myra spoke in unison, and Myra said, 'We were just going to suggest it, and you're coming to stay with us until you're really yourself again.'

Lisa tried to protest, but Myra was adamant. 'Yes, you must. I don't want you to be alone in the flat, and Dinah's tour has been extended, so she's off again. We'd love to have you.'

Lisa submitted. She would only brood if she went back to the empty flat, she knew, but no one could surrender to the doldrums in Jos and Myra's lively but haphazard environment.

'I'll have a word with Dr Simms,' she said.

'And we'll be back first thing in the morning to collect you,' Myra promised. She grinned down at Lisa. 'Anyway, you've got to come because we told Joseph we'd be bringing you back, and there'll be hell to pay if we turn up without Auntie Lisa after all.'

'Where is Joseph?' Lisa glanced around, as if there was the remotest chance of concealing a lively two-year-old in the room.

'Oh, I left him with his godmother,' Myra said comfortably. 'He had a bit of a cold, so I thought it best not to bring him.' She shivered. 'You know what they say about the frozen north!'

Lisa felt perceptibly happier after Jos and Myra had departed. She got out of bed, and sat by the window for a while. She had been up for a time each day, and had been amazed how shaky her legs felt when she tried to move about. The nurses had said it was reaction, and she didn't doubt they were right.

Presently she sounded a buzzer, and when one of the nurses appeared, she said that she would be leaving in the morning, and would like to have a bath.

The girl looked taken aback and began to say something about Dr Simms, but Lisa merely repeated that she would be leaving, and reiterated her request for a bath, and eventually the girl grudgingly agreed.

'But you're very pale,' she said. 'Would you like me to help you?'

'No, thank you,' Lisa said politely.

On her way to the bathroom, she heard two of the other staff discussing Jos's visit. There'd been a programme about him on television that they had seen, and they thought he was a glamorous figure, but they couldn't figure Myra out, or what part Lisa played in it all.

'Doesn't his wife mind?' one of them wondered, and Lisa suppressed a rueful smile.

'Not in the least,' she said as she passed the office door, and heard a muffled gasp of embarrassment.

The bath felt wonderful, and it was good to dress herself in her own things instead of the hospital gown with its tapes. She could have asked for them before, she supposed, but nothing had seemed to matter very much.

The nurse had been right, though, she thought studying herself critically. She did look pale. There was no sign now of that embryo Caribbean tan she had brought with her. The angles of her face were altogether too sharply defined, and her eyes looked enormous. I look like a hungry cat outside a closed door, she thought, her mouth twisting wryly.

But of course that was exactly what she had become, and all that she hungered for was closed away from her for ever.

On her way back from the bathroom, she paused outside Julie's door, with its neat card 'Miss Riderwood', but she made no attempt to go in or even to knock.

'Goodbye, Julie. Be happy, please be happy,' she said silently, and turned away.

After a week at Jos and Myra's, Lisa had begun to look as well as feel better. Myra was a lavish if unpredictable cook, generous with wine and herbs and second helpings. Her family thrived on it, and she was determined that Lisa was going to thrive too.

She would soon be ready to start work again, she thought, and she told Jos so, but all he said was, 'Take it easy, love,' so she guessed she hadn't totally regained her looks.

She had discarded the sticking plaster, and the faint mark on her forehead could be hidden by her hair, so that wasn't a problem, but she couldn't disguise the haunted look in her eyes. It was there, and Jos knew it because he was a photographer and an artist and he was trained to look out for such things. If he photographed her now, it wouldn't be as the Amber Girl, she knew.

In the meantime, it was pleasant to help Myra in her periodic bouts of tidying the tall Victorian house they lived in, and to play with little Joseph, and to talk to Myra's girl friends when they dropped in for coffee, or the more cosmopolitan crowd who came for dinner or drinks in the evenings. It was like being part of a family again, but without the aggro, the tensions of Stoniscliffe.

Of course, there wasn't a moment of the day or night when she didn't think of him. She could not get that last image out of her mind—the bitter accusation in his eyes as he watched James half-weeping across her bed, and then the door closing shutting her off from him.

What a fool she had been ever to imagine, to dream that things could ever be any different between them, she thought wearily, wondering what his reaction would have been to the news that she had gone off to London with yet another married man, because as luck would have it Jos had arrived alone to pick her up from the hospital, and they had collected Myra from the hotel afterwards.

She was sitting in the big untidy kitchen one afternoon watching Myra prepare goulash while Joseph made an indescribable mess with his finger paints when Myra said, 'Simon's coming to dinner tonight. I hope you don't mind. He's been hinting for an invitation ever since he heard you were here.'

Lisa shrugged. Simon was the least of her problems. 'Of course I don't mind.'

Myra sent her a quizzical glance. 'That's what I thought. Poor Simon! Or should I say poor Lisa?'

Lisa summoned a smile. 'Stupid Lisa, maybe. I must be a fool to let Simon slip through my fingers. After all, my looks won't last for ever, and modelling is a young girl's game.'

'Oh, to hell with Simon.' Myra dismissed him with an airy wave of her cooking spoon. 'It's this other man I'm interested in—the one who makes you look like death when you think no one's noticing. You may not know it, love, but every so often you drift into a little private reverie, and I can't believe it's pleasant.'

Lisa chewed her bottom lip. 'It isn't. I—I can't talk about it, Myra. I'd like to, and one day perhaps I'll be able to, but not now.'

Myra smiled at her warmly. 'Any time, love. Oh God, Joseph, you're supposed to put the paint on the paper, not your face! Look at him, Lisa. He looks like Sitting Bull!'

Simon wasn't intended to be the only guest, but the couple who had also been invited rang up to say they had baby-sitting problems, so that was how it turned out.

He arrived smiling, with a bottle of wine, but underneath was a man with a grievance.

He said, 'Hello, lovely stranger,' to Lisa and kissed her,

but there was an edge to his words, and his mouth bare▌
grazed the cheek she offered him.

She said levelly, 'Hello, Simon.'

The food was delicious, and it should have been ▌
pleasant occasion, yet it wasn't. When dinner was ove▌
Jos and Myra excused themselves on the grounds ▌
washing up, and Simon and Lisa were left alone in th▌
sitting room on the first floor.

Simon said tautly, 'Enjoying your stay here?'

'Very much.' He couldn't make any capital out of th▌
surely, Lisa thought.

'Jos and Myra went to the hospital to bring you home▌
understand.' Simon picked up his brandy glass and dran▌
'It didn't occur to you to ask me to do so.'

'To be frank, no, it didn't.'

'No,' he said bitterly. 'It's been weeks, Lisa, and no▌
word, not a sign from you. That shows me very plainly h▌
little I figure in your life.'

'I wasn't aware that you wanted anything else.' Th▌
wasn't altogether true, she thought guiltily, but it gave h▌
an opportunity to escape from this situation with digni▌

'Oh, God!' he burst out. 'You know—you must know h▌
I feel about you. If you'd only asked me I'd have come fr▌
the ends of the earth to bring you back to London. Eve▌
those dreadful stories in the papers had been true, I'd s▌
have wanted you.'

Lisa supposed he must be sincere, but the drama in ▌
voice, the high-flown words were just an embarrassmen▌

She heard herself say weakly, 'I didn't know. I thou▌
we were friends. Can't we be friends?'

'I want more from you than that, Lisa,' he said thick▌
'Much, much more.' He got up as he spoke, knocking ▌
remains of his brandy over Myra's rug.

Lisa leapt up too. 'Oh heavens, I'd better get a cloth ▌

The sitting room, alone with Simon, suddenly no lon▌

seemed a good place to be. She wished Jos and Myra would come with the coffee.

'Leave the bloody rug,' Simon said violently. 'Myras will never notice.'

So much for his kind hostess, Lisa thought, taking a step backwards. Simon came after her, wrapping his arms around her and pulling her close to him. His breath was hot on her averted face.

He said hoarsely, 'Don't treat me like a stranger, Lisa. I've played it cool because I thought that was what you wanted, but we can't go on like this. You're so beautiful. I want you—I've got to have you!'

His mouth fastened on hers with a greed that made her recoil, and his hands fumbled at her breasts.

When she could speak, she gasped, 'Simon—for God's sake!' but he seemed oblivious. Somewhere dimly she thought she heard the sound of the doorbell, and she could only pray it was the Jeffersons, who had said they might come round later if they could find another baby-sitter. Someone had to come, to rescue her from this nightmare. She had never dreamed she would have to fight Simon off, but he seemed totally out of control, bent mindlessly on the gratification of his own desires and fantasies.

There were footsteps approaching, and Myra's voice saying, 'In there,' and half delirious with relief, Lisa thought, 'The cavalry to the rescue!' and blessed the unknown Jeffersons.

As the door opened Simon let her go so abruptly that she almost stumbled, and stood glaring at the doorway.

He demanded belligerently, 'Who the hell are you?'

'My name's Riderwood,' Dane said quietly. 'I'm clearly interrupting something, and I'm sorry. I'll go.'

'No.' Lisa thought she screamed the word, but it came out as a strangled croak. 'No—don't go, please!'

She could imagine what she looked like. Half the buttons

on her silk shirt were open, and her hair which had been pinned up on top of her head at the start of the evening was now festooned around her neck. She understood now why Julie took refuge in hysterics. It would have been nice to lie down on the carpet and drum her heels and scream.

Simon said thickly, 'What the hell is this? Riderwood. That's the name of the people Lisa was staying with in Yorkshire. Are you one of them?'

'Yes.' Dane had come further into the room, and was watching Simon levelly, his hands on his hips.

'Oh, I see,' Simon sneered. 'God, do I see! No wonder there was never a message, never a phone call. No wonder suddenly didn't exist!' He laughed harshly, observing the sudden flare of colour in Lisa's face, and the way she pressed her hands to her burning cheeks. 'God, what a fool I've been! Well, here she is, friend. The beautiful Lisa Grayson —all yours. And I hope you get more mileage out of her than I have, the frigid little bitch,' he added with total vindictiveness.

Dane hit him, and he stumbled backwards falling into one of the chairs, nursing his jaw and staring up almost in credulously.

Dane said brusquely, 'Don't be here when I come back.' He took Lisa's arm and hauled her unceremoniously out of the room. He said, 'Where can we talk?'

It was a big house. It was full of rooms. They could have been alone in almost all of them, but she could only stare at him mutely.

He muttered, 'Oh God,' and opened the nearest door, pushing her inside. It was the family bathroom, and Myra had filled it with plants and cane furniture. Dane pulled forward a high-backed chair and Lisa sank down on to it.

He said, 'That, dare I presume, was Simon?'

She nodded.

'When I came in you were fighting him off, or trying to

e remarked. 'What with that, and his final unpleasant remark, can I infer that you're not living with him?'

'Does it matter?' She was beginning to recover the
owers of speech.

'Oh yes, it matters very much. Look at me, Lisa.'

She had been staring down at her hands which were
lenched together in her lap, but now she raised her eyes
arily to his face.

She said slowly, 'How did you know where I was?'

'I didn't, but the hospital was agog over the fact that
ou'd left for London with Jos Temple, so when you weren't
the flat, I decided to come and ask him.' His face was
ddenly taut and rather grim, and she flinched instinctively.
or a moment he stared at her as if he didn't believe it,
en he said with immense weariness, 'Have I really
ightened you so much, Lisa? I've come here to try and
ake my peace with you, if that's possible.' His mouth
isted ruefully. 'Can I admit that Mrs Temple was a
rprise to me, and leave it at that.'

'As I said before, does it matter? You've always thought
e worst of me, Dane. You can believe what you like
out Jos and me.'

He said, 'Believing the worst of you was a habit I got into.
was easy at first. I was an arrogant young fool, and I
ented anyone taking my mother's place. But no one
ld resent Jennifer for long. Knowing her turned out to
a privilege. But you were a different matter because you
ented me too, and that was a challenge in a way. And then
e day I came back and you weren't a sullen child any
re. You were almost a woman, and you were going to be
utiful. You were at the dawn of that beauty, and that's
y I bought you that record for your birthday. I tried to tell
self I was pleased because I was going to have two good-
king sisters, but it didn't work. As time went on, I had to
e to terms with the truth—that I wasn't your brother,

and I certainly didn't want you as any kind of sister.'

'But you wanted me,' she said coolly and clearly. '
think you established that beyond reasonable doubt. An
you had me.'

It was his turn to flinch, she saw with astonishment.

'Yes, I did, God forgive me. I don't expect you to. Every
thing was wrong about the way I treated you. It's haunted m
ever since—the way you were with me—your apparent in
nocence. I told myself it wasn't possible because I couldn
face the other implication—that you'd been a virgin, an
that I'd ruined everything for you—for both of us. But I hav
to face it now, Lisa. Is it true? Was I the first with you

She closed her eyes. 'Yes.'

'Oh God,' he muttered softly, and there was a long silenc
Then he said huskily, 'I should have known. I should hav
realised, but I was too angry, too jealous to think of anythir
except that I wanted you. It was only later when I allowe
myself to think about what had happened that I realise
that no one with the kind of experience I'd credited yo
with could have been so frightened and bewildered b
passion—even the brutal kind I'd shown you.' He pause
'I came back to see you, to try to talk the thing out,
see if I could mend things between us—but you'd gone.'

Lisa said between stiff lips, 'And of course you couldr
have come after me.'

'I could have,' he said grimly, 'if it hadn't been for th
European sales tour I was committed to. I'd always made
rule that I never let my personal life get in the way of wor
Things weren't too healthy at Riderwoods just then, a
Chas was working like a dog too in the States. But
promised myself when the tour was over, I'd find you.'

'But you didn't.'

He looked at her levelly. 'By the time I came back, you
become the Amber Girl. Those bloody photographs w
everywhere. Every time I opened a newspaper, th

eemed to be an item in a gossip column about you, linking
ou with some man or another. I had to concede that my
nstincts about you had probably been wrong after all.'
Ie added flatly, 'And I was angry because your departure had
urt Chas and Julie. I felt that you'd betrayed them. Chas
ad treated you as if you were his own child, and Julie
epended on you in so many ways, and you'd left them.'

'But I had to go,' she whispered.

'Because I forced you to?' He gave a slight groan. 'I was
alfway to Leeds when it suddenly occurred to me that you
ight run away again. There was no logic in it, but I
iddenly knew I couldn't allow it to happen again, so I
ame back, and there you were in Julie's car. It was like
repeat of a nightmare, and when she turned the thing
ver in that ditch, I was nearly demented.' He shook his
ead, remembering. 'I pulled you out, and there was blood
a your face. It wasn't until the ambulance arrived that I
alised it was Julie who was in urgent need of medical
tention. And then I was angry again, because I thought
u'd made her take a chance and drive too fast.'

Lisa felt as if she was dreaming. It was all so totally
areal. She gripped the canework on the chair, letting
leave its imprint on her flesh. What was she doing in this
ant-filled, slightly steamy room, with its exotic jungle
allpaper and cavernous bath with Myra's carefully applied
encils along the sides? How was it possible that she was
re with Dane, and that he could be talking about anger,
d yet not angry? It was ridiculous, ludicrous, and a wild
bble of laughter welled up inside her.

There was a sharp stinging pain across her cheek, and
e sank back in the chair gasping.

'That's enough,' Dane said crisply. 'I've had enough
steria from Julie over the past few days to last me a life-
e.'

'You slapped me,' she protested half tearfully.

'And presently I'll kiss you.' His hand cupped her chin and he looked at her mouth as if it was some rare and precious flower.

She said breathlessly, 'How—how is Julie? Is she still in hospital?'

'No, she took a leaf out of your book and discharged herself. She and James Dalton are now occupying a bed sitting room in Leeds and behaving like the leads in a Shakespearean tragedy,' he said sardonically.

Lisa's lips parted in astonishment. 'Don't you care?'

'Of course I care. Julie's my sister. I hadn't figured her a home-wrecker—not that James and Celia ever had much a home to wreck. And what Julie and he have going for them apart from a conviction that they're the original star-crossed lovers seems strictly limited.' Dane sounded weary. ' seems they plan to go and live in Africa, and as far as I' concerned it can't be too soon.'

'How has Chas taken the news?' Lisa asked quickly.

'Better than any of us could have hoped. He has unexpected streak of resilience.' He paused. 'And he need it, because Julie told us everything.'

'Everything?'

He nodded slowly. 'From the way you'd always shield her at school, right through to her involvement with t Hammonds and the way she tried to disguise her affair w Dalton. Every last detail, including how you'd begged her slow down before the crash. A lot of it wasn't very e to stomach, especially for my father. But neither he Julie know the real damage that was done—the damag us.'

There was a silence, then Lisa said, 'So now you kn Is that what you've come all this way to tell me?'

'Not just that. I came to ask why? Why in the hell you take the blame for Julie's stupidity? When I accused you, why didn't you tell me the truth?'

She lifted a shoulder helplessly. 'Would you have believed me?'

'Perhaps not immediately, but I would have been bound to check on what you'd said. God knows Julie needed to be stopped in her tracks. We've all given way to her too often in the past, partly because of her temperament. She's been worrying Chas for years, apparently. I'm not making excuses for her, but perhaps if we'd all got together years ago and put our cards on the table, then at least we could have saved ourselves this scandal over her cold-blooded plan to marry Tony Bainbridge.'

'How could I have said anything?' she sighed. 'Chas treated me as a daughter, yes, but to you I was always the outsider, the intruder. You and Chas and Julie were the Riderwoods, a closed circle I couldn't break into. I couldn't do anything that might damage that circle—repay Chas's kindness to me by destroying his faith in his own child.'

'So instead you chose to destroy our faith in you,' he said. 'Oh God, you little fool!' He hesitated. 'I had another reason for coming here. I'm asking you to forgive me, Lisa, for everything I've said and done to hurt you, for every unjustified thought I've ever harboured against you. I'm prepared to ask for your forgiveness on my knees if it's necessary, if that's what you want. And I want you to come back to Stoniscliffe. Chas needs you.'

Lisa shook her head. 'I can't go back there.'

He was silent for a moment, then he rose from the half-kneeling position he had adopted beside the chair and moved away.

He said quietly, 'So you can't forgive me. Would it influence your decision if I told you I was prepared to move out?'

The deep inner pain had returned, so sharp and fierce that it seemed to be tearing her apart.

She bent her head, allowing her dishevelled hair to fall

across her face. 'That—wouldn't make any difference.'

She heard him sigh, then he said, 'I see. I'm sorry, Lisa. I can tell I've upset you, and that was the last thing I intended. I'll go.'

Lisa thought in anguish, 'He'll go, and I'll never see him again.'

She heard a voice she hardly recognised say, 'You said you were going to kiss me.'

Dane was at the door, his hand already on the knob, but as she spoke he turned sharply. Two long strides and he was lifting her up out of the chair, and his mouth was on hers, fiercely and achingly possessive. She clung to him, the tears which she had dammed back, spilling down her face as she responded with her whole heart to the demands of his kiss.

He tore his lips from hers at last with something like a groan and imprisoned her face between his hands, staring down at her fiercely.

He said, 'I don't care how many men there've been in your life, Lisa. I was the first and I'm going to be the last. You belong to me, and I'm never going to let you go again. We're going back to Yorkshire tomorrow.'

She tried to smile. 'Because Chas needs me?'

'Because I need you. Because we're going to be married, and give the local gossips something to chew on apart from James and Julie. We've wasted two years out of our lives and I'm damned if we're going to waste any more.'

Lisa gave an unsteady laugh. 'What will Chas say? And—Tina?'

His mouth twisted slightly. 'Tina is unimportant—a charming diversion who totally failed to take my mind off you. No one ever succeeded in doing that. As for Chas—he already has the champagne on ice. He told me not to come back without you.'

'Oh!' Lisa gasped. 'So you were that sure of me?'

'I wasn't sure of you at all,' Dane said quietly, and looking into his eyes, she saw an uncertainty, a new vulnerability which twisted her heart. 'I didn't even know if you'd give me a hearing, or if I could make you understand how I felt—that I was asking for much, much more than your forgiveness. And all the time you sat in that damned chair, like a little ghost, hardly saying a word.'

'I was waiting for one word that showed you cared,' she said. 'I knew you wanted me, but that wasn't enough. I always wanted you to love me, even when I was a child and thought I hated you. One word of praise from you made my heart sing. That's why I said I couldn't go back to Stoniscliffe. I'd have died rather than lived under the same roof as you again under the old footing.'

Dane said slowly, 'I know I've waited too long to say it, Lisa, but I love you. It's a cliché to say you always hurt the one you love, but in our case it's been true. But I'll make it up to you, darling, if it takes the rest of our lives.'

'I think I'll like that.' Smiling, she slid her arms up round his neck, glorying in her new-found power over him. 'This is the first time I've ever been proposed to in a bathroom!'

'Where did Simon propose?' His voice was still quiet.

'He didn't. I always tried never to let any of my—relationships get to that stage. It never seemed fair.' She hesitated. 'You heard what he said—that I was frigid. Well, in a way it's been true. I never wanted anyone to touch or kiss me—after you. I blamed you for that—blamed what had happened between us. I told myself you'd stopped me from fulfilling myself as a woman. So there was never anyone. You wanted to be the first and the last. Well, you are, my darling. The first, the last and the only man in my life.'

He looked at her for a long time, then he said huskily, 'I don't deserve that.'

He kissed her again, his lips caressing hers with all the

sweetness and tenderness she had ever longed for, filling her with a soaring delight.

There had been darkness, and bitterness, but they would be forgotten, and soon, very soon, there would be another summer dawn.

Harlequin Plus

THE HAUNTING MUSIC OF RAVEL

Maurice Joseph Ravel, a French composer who is a favorite of Sara Craven's heroine, is best loved for his haunting and hypnotic musical compositions.

Born in 1875 in the Basque region of France, he made his debut as a composer in 1898 in Paris, and his early works were praised for "opening up a new world of haunting sounds."

In 1912 the celebrated Ballet Russe de Monte Carlo presented what is generally regarded as Ravel's greatest work—*Daphnis et Chloë*—praised for its exquisite beauty and magic. Yet despite this and several other fine compositions, Ravel was not taking the world by storm.

That changed with his composition *Bolero* which, when introduced in Paris in 1928, caused a sensation. A compelling theme that moves relentlessly to a tremendous crescendo, *Bolero* received acclaim wherever presented, and Ravel became the most sought-after composer in France. Recently the piece enjoyed renewed popularity, its rising rhythm featured prominently in the sound track of the movie *10*.

On a personal level, Ravel has been described as a man of meticulous manners. He never married, but lived with a family of Siamese cats, whom he talked to in a "cat language" he insisted they understood.

Maurice Ravel died in Paris in 1937 of a brain disorder. His legacy is a varied collection of rich and original works. As the composer himself once explained, "I belong to no school of music. I try to create beautiful ideas in music. Great music must always come from the heart; great music must always be beautiful."

FREE!

A hardcover Romance Treasury volume
containing 3 treasured works of romance
by 3 outstanding Harlequin authors . . .

. . as your introduction to Harlequin's
Romance Treasury subscription plan!

Romance Treasury

. . almost 600 pages of exciting romance reading
every month at the low cost of $6.97 a volume!

A wonderful way to collect many of Harlequin's most beautiful love
stories, all originally published in the late '60s and early '70s.
Each value-packed volume, bound in a distinctive gold-embossed
leatherette case and wrapped in a colorfully illustrated dust jacket,
contains . . .
3 full-length novels by 3 world-famous authors of romance fiction
a unique illustration for every novel
the elegant touch of a delicate bound-in ribbon bookmark . . .
and much, much more!

Romance Treasury

. . for a library of romance you'll treasure forever!

Complete and mail today the FREE gift certificate and subscription
reservation on the following page.